HAUNTINGS

AND OTHER TALES OF DANGER, LOVE, AND SOMETIMES LOSS

HAUNTINGS

AND OTHER TALES OF DANGER,
LOVE, AND SOMETIMES LOSS

BETSY HEARNE

GREENWILLOW BOOKS
An Imprint of HarperCollins*Publishers*

Hauntings: And Other Tales of Danger, Love, and Sometimes Loss

The lines of verse quoted on p. 136 are from Joyce Kilmer, "Trees," *Poetry* (1913); and Ogden Nash, "Song of the Open Road," *Many Long Years Ago* (Boston: Little, Brown, 1945).

The text of this book is set in 12-point Meridien Roman.
Book design by Paul Zakris.

Library of Congress Cataloging-in-Publication Data
Hearne, Betsy Gould.
Hauntings, and other tales of danger, love, and sometimes
loss / by Betsy Hearne.
　p. cm.
"Greenwillow Books."
Summary: Fifteen stories of death and hauntings, set in the past, the
present, and the afterlife.
ISBN-13: 978-0-06-123910-6 (trade bdg.)　ISBN-10: 0-06-123910-0 (trade bdg.)
ISBN-13: 978-0-06-123911-3 (lib. bdg.)　ISBN-10: 0-06-123911-9 (lib. bdg.)
[1. Children's stories, American. 2. Death—Juvenile fiction. 3. Death—Fiction.
4. Supernatural—Fiction. 5. Short stories.] I. Title.
PZ7.H3464 Hau 2007 [Fic] 22　2006033711

First Edition　10 9 8 7 6 5 4 3 2 1

Greenwillow Books

To Michael Eugene Patrick Claffey, *cushla machree*

PREFACE

Hauntings don't always involve terror or ghoulish apparitions. We are all haunted by something, whether it's worries or wishes or great mysteries like love and death. The old days hosted otherworldly beings in the shape of magical creatures, ghosts, and strange visitors. Today's unsettling encounters are just as common if not so visible. The stories in the first section here reflect folkways, mainly from Ireland, where Celtic lore developed some irresistibly eerie themes. The second section moves across the Atlantic Ocean, as did so many immigrants, and reveals newer aspects of visitation. The third section . . . well, you'll see.

PART I

THE PAST

(SET MOSTLY IN IRELAND)

✝RYS✝

To bind her breasts she needed no candlelight
but deftly, in the dark, wound strips of torn sheet
tight against the rounds of flesh. Her shirt lay flat
then, and the jacket after it. She tightened a
leather belt to keep the breeches from slipping
down her hips and last tucked a pistol into the
belt, a knife down the side of her boot, and her
long black braid under a three-cornered hat. She
crept down the back stairs, unlocked the door,
and saddled the mare while her master and mis-
tress snored in tandem. *The hour was late*.

The hour was late. He and his old horse were
tired, but coveting the ale and oats of home,
they hurried on. He had been well warned not

to ride overnight, but a young man thought nothing of danger. He had, after all, been alive his whole life and couldn't imagine the world otherwise. If he was aware of anything besides hunger and wind in his face, it was the desperate need for *a kiss*.

A kiss could be the culprit of his delay. She imagined him now in the city taverns, night after night, week after week, month after month, staying for kisses from one or another of the loose (or, worse, not loose) women on the lookout for a young man of his bearing. Although he had pledged his love and she had given him a gold ring to seal it, who knew what a ring meant these days? She'd stolen the ring on her first raid (and told him it was her mother's), but its value was certain. She was good at *getting gold*.

Getting gold was growing on his mind. What could he offer her? He was poor, but his search for work had failed. He seemed to have talent for nothing, and certainly no schooling. His slim build boded well for love but ill for *heavy labor*.

* * *

Heavy labor was not to her liking. She shunned the servant jobs in the manor. To hell with their highborn ways. Still, a lass must eat—and satisfy herself in other things—so this job suited her well. May her dead parents forgive her and her foster folk never guess *the truth*.

The truth shook him like a terrier with a rat. She would hate him for his defeat. Even as he hurtled toward her, he could hear the scorn in her voice. He could hear something else as well, *the sound of other hoofbeats*.

The sound of other hoofbeats brought her to a halt. So soon a victim comes? She wheeled her horse behind some trees that shaded the plain by day and shadowed it by night. Yes, someone was coming. May he be rich and easily disarmed. She pulled a black mask over her black eyes, *waiting*.

Waiting was out of the question. He had promised her marriage and freedom from orphaned bondage. But how can a poor young man support a wife, especially one with expensive tastes like hers? Ah, but the taste of her. He must somehow *stand and deliver*.

Stand and deliver, she shouted in the deep voice she had practiced so often and well. Her horse blocked his own, which whinnied and turned aside, its flanks steaming. Only then did she know him, but never paused. She held the pistol steady toward his heart and called, *Your money or your life*.

Your money or your life, indeed, he laughed. I can offer you neither, for money have I none and my life is worth nothing *without it*.

Without it you shall be, she declared, unless you hand over the gold I see glinting on your finger. Her own black-gloved hand absorbed the moonlight. Only the pistol gleamed. Yet he seemed fearless and even fairer than she remembered. Anger over his long absence drove her. Coldly she demanded again, *The ring*.

The ring, he answered, is not mine to give. It is a gift of trust from someone dear. Kill me if you will, but when you take this ring from my dead hand, my ghost will hunt you down. So take it at your *peril.*

Peril is of little concern to me, sir, but your words reveal a loyal heart. Perhaps your life is worth something after all. What can you offer in lieu of the ring? She waved the pistol once more and saw him reach for *the pocket watch.*

The pocket watch fit smooth in his hand. He'd been tempted to pawn it but never succumbed. Now he threw it and could not help but marvel at the thief's neat catch of it *midair.*

Midair she dropped the reins and snatched the watch in its fall. Both hands were full, one with a weapon and the other with her haul. She held to the horse with tightened knees and turned it with a nudge of spur. Beware of following me, she growled, and dropped the watch in her greatcoat pocket. You're lucky your nag is too slow to steal. Then she disappeared into the dark. She must head away and double back to sneak her own horse into the barn and herself into bed. The foster folks' farm was lonely, and no one would see her from *the village*.

The village was quiet when finally he made his way there. At the innkeeper's stable he tended the horse and lay down in the stall beside it. A tavern boy he had been and a tavern boy he'd always be. As surely as the sun rose now and every day, the innkeeper would enslave him for the loan he could not repay. And his father's watch gone, now, to a highwayman. So much for *venturing forth*.

Venturing forth to rob made her late to rise, but the children soon pummeled her awake. Lazy creature, they screamed, our mother needs you, get up, get up. Like lice they squirmed over her. It would be evening before she could leave again, this time forever. She had only been waiting *his return*.

His return was cause for much jeering by the innkeeper, but he held his peace and bowed his head. His only thought was seeing her one last time, yet he dreaded to see her, too, for the pain it would bring. Still the day passed, as days will, and suddenly she was there in the garden with a welcoming smile and a toss of her head and a long sweet kiss beside the rosebushes. What news, she asked, whereupon the pocket watch swung free on its chain from the folds of *her loosened cloak.*

Her loosened cloak drew his eye to the golden watch, and his face turned rosy red. Ah my dear, she said, don't blush at so silly a thing. 'Twas I who robbed you on the plain, but now I've brought you back your watch again and more, a store of gold and all my gear—for you've proved true and beyond that, brave. She touched his ring and pulled him toward the stable door. He took a better horse this time, one to match her own, and they raced each other off into *the gloom.*

The gloom still echoes with hoofbeats, say those who hear them now, though the tryst is centuries old. No one knows how the lovers fared, after they ran away, but tales of highway robbers ride the land to this very day. *Listen.*

Listen.

FORTRESS

Before he was eighteen he could build anything, and there was much to build. Every chief and lord and king must have a castle, every clan a tower. Every stone must be levered and hauled and chiseled and fitted for every hall and hearth, the wood for every door hewn.

The house he built for himself was humble, but it was built with love for the woman he would marry. Even at seventeen, she hadn't the prettiest face in the village, but she was quick-witted and kind and just as he could build anything, she could make anything grow—the healthiest chicken or lamb or goat, the loveliest flower, the strongest herb, the sweetest carrot. "She could plant a nail in the ground," he said, "and it would come up a hammer." She had a way with her, and her ways pleased him. The priest who married them had heard many a pair swear "till death do us part," but between these two he saw an uncommon bond.

Yet no love is without its quarrels, and their first was their worst. It came unexpected like a storm from the south. "Good news," he said one night at supper. "There's a fortress to be built for Lord Ragnall, and I've been summoned to build it."

Her eyes darkened. "Lord Ragnall is a hard man," she said, "quick to anger and quicker to strike."

"But this will be the making of me," he said.

"It will be the breaking of you."

"Don't be foolish," he said.

"Don't go," she said. "Say you won't."

"I must," he said.

"No."

"Yes."

"NO!"

Those were the last words they spoke at supper, or the whole evening long, or the next day, till she could bear it no longer. Seeing him gather his tools to go, she flung herself on him with a cry and he closed his arms around her. She shook her head and clung to him tighter. That night he blew out the bedside candle, melting into the precious glass candlestick she had from her grandmother, and made up for their disagreement a hundred times over.

After that it was away with him, over the mountains and far on, where he worked from dawn to dark, never complaining though Lord Ragnall drove him as a hunter runs his prey to the ground, demanding secret passages so well hidden that no enemy could ever trap the lord in his own lair, designing a false door facing the sea cliff where Lord Ragnall could lead unwelcome guests, step aside, and push them to their deaths on the rocks below. In sun and wind, in rain and frost, the foundation and walls of the fortress grew.

Waiting at home, she grew big with their first child, and grew peas and cabbages and milked the goat, and hoped he would be home when the child was born. But her neighbors and an old midwife delivered the boy in his absence, and now she worked twice as hard as before but with better company than he had, for the baby was calm and cheerful while Lord Ragnall was dour and grim.

The boy took his first step and spoke his first word, and many more of both, before the day came when the fortress was all but finished. Lord Ragnall called his builder to him for the last payment but locked the door with only the two of them there.

"You will find the work well done," said the builder. "There will never be another like it."

"No, there will not," said Lord Ragnall, and he drew his sword with its edges of sharpened steel. "You have indeed built the fortress well, but you know its secrets too well."

"I and those who worked with me," said the builder.

"Each knows but one secret. You know them all," said Lord Ragnall.

"There is one other thing that I know and you do not."

"And what is that?" asked Lord Ragnall as he paced closer to the builder.

"The spell I must put upon the place, against attack."

"A spell," mocked Lord Ragnall. "There is no

magic in fire and force—only blood will do," and he took another step.

"What of Dun An Oir, that fell to a few with all its might, and none could tell why? What of Duneen and Dun Aeongus and Dun Manus?"

"The element of surprise," said Lord Ragnall. "Or betrayal, or perhaps a secret too well known."

"Or perhaps not," said the builder. "It will cost you nothing to be sure and could cost you much to spurn my warning."

"Then make your magic now, builder, and perhaps I'll spare your life."

"I cannot."

"And why, pray tell, is that?"

"I must have my glass hammer."

"Glass hammer!" bellowed Lord Ragnall. "Now you jest. A hammer of glass? You think I'd let you slip away with such a ruse?"

"Then send someone to fetch it from my wife."

"And trust this great secret of yours to a chain of gossips?"

"Send your own son. My wife will tell no one if she knows it means my life."

"That it does," said Lord Ragnall.

"I know that it does," said the builder, and thought to himself, He means to kill me either way, but perhaps there is some small hope.

Now Lord Ragnall's son was young but trained in his father's cruelty, and his lip curled as he learned of this fool's errand. Yet he went nonetheless, thinking of the young wife and what he could do to her once he got what his father wanted. So he drove his handsome horse over the mountains and far on till it foamed, and when he came to the builder's house he hurled himself at her door and pounded it with a hard fist.

She opened it, startled, a child on one hip, and stared at him wide-eyed. "My husband," she said before he could speak. "Is all well?"

"He is in need of something to finish the task," said Lord Ragnall's son roughly.

"And what is that?" she asked, holding the squirming boy tighter to her.

"He claims to need a glass hammer, a hammer of glass," sneered Lord Ragnall's son.

"Ah," she said, and stared past him into the clouding sky as if she would melt into it.

"Well?" he demanded.

"His hammer of glass?" she asked.

"So I said, or so he says."

"Then it must be the one he keeps upstairs," she said at last, and turned away.

He seized her arm and shook her till the child's head fell back and forth. "None of your tricks," he growled.

"No," she said, and pulled her arm free and placed the child in his tall cradle, the one crafted by her husband to hold all their children to come. "Wait here," she crooned to the boy, and smoothed his hair.

"I will come with you," said Lord Ragnall's son.

"Yes," she said, and climbed the stairs that were cut and pegged by her husband, and saw Lord Ragnall's son glance at the bed that was shaped and smoothed to a silken finish by her husband, and knew what Lord Ragnall's son would do to her on that bed.

"There," she said, pointing at the huge locked chest, squared and hinged by her husband with the strongest leather, to hold the goose-feather quilts she had spread on the hedge to air. "He keeps the glass hammer locked away."

"Then unlock it, woman," commanded Lord Ragnall's son.

Slowly she went to the chimney stones, warm in the winter, cool now in the breezes of spring that stroked the hawthorn blooming white in the fields outside, and the foxglove nodding along the lanes, and the roses tumbling over the garden wall. She slipped her fingers into a thin crack and pulled out the key, turned toward the dark corner where the chest stood, bent to unlock it, and felt his hot breath on her neck as he crept behind her.

"There," she said again, pointing into the chest, and stepped sideways. "You can take it yourself."

He leaned down, straining to see in the dim corners. "There's nothing," he snarled, "but an empty wooden chest."

"Look closer," she said softly, "the glass hammer is not easily seen," and as he leaned down farther she seized the heavy glass candlestick beside the bed and brought it down on the back of his head. He fell forward without a sound, and she folded his limp form into the chest, banged down the lid, and turned the key in the iron lock.

"There," she said a third time. "Thank your stars that my good husband drilled holes for the quilts to breathe." Then she sent back Lord Ragnall's son's handsome horse with a slap to its rear and a message tied to its reins, *My husband for your son*, and she hid herself and the child among kinfolk who would protect her. A day went by and she waited. Another day came, and with it her husband, walking wearily down the road. After looking to see he was not followed, she came out of hiding and ran to him.

"You guessed the glass hammer," he said, drawing her close, together with his son.

"I guessed it and used it," she answered.

From that day on, the builder and his wife rarely had an ill-tempered word for each other, but it was not so for Lord Ragnall nor for his son, who returned to the fortress with a knot on his head and anger on his tongue. As happens in a house built of fear, he and his father feuded and fell out, and finally the fortress itself fell—perhaps from force, or by the element of surprise, or betrayal, or secrets too well known, or the storms of time, or perhaps because it was never shielded by magic made with a glass hammer.

The builder became famous throughout Ireland as the Gobán Saor, the Master Builder, whose descendants fill houses everywhere, but the fortress lies a heap of haunted stones as cold as the hearts of Lord Ragnall and his son.

Lost

Danno scraped fallen leaves aside, looking for the wild mushrooms that sprang up overnight, white on top, brown underneath, with a taste that put potatoes to shame. You had to take care—there were mushrooms with poison enough to kill—but Danno was careful in all things. As he walked slowly through the woods beside the field, adding mushrooms to his pouch here and there, he all at once saw something glinting in the grass and stooped to pick it up. Marvelous to behold, it was a golden ball, small enough to fit in the palm of his hand. Now, he thought, what a nest egg this will be, and he took it home and hid it away in the niche beside his fireplace. To be sure no one stole his treasure, he took some mortar and sealed the niche with a stone.

It was not long after that, on a late summer day when the sun heated the heather, that a young woman surprised Danno in his own front yard. Lovely she was, with dark hair curling around her face and a bloom on her cheeks. Danno, a bachelor so shy he could never look a female in the eye, doffed his hat to her, but it was she who spoke the first word.

"I wonder," she said, "if you would know of anyone hereabouts who needs some cooking and cleaning done, for I've lost my place in service to wealthy folk far from here and have lost my way as well."

"Aye," said Danno after a pause, and didn't he amaze himself by asking her in, like a man charmed, and striking a bargain on the spot that she would keep house for him at a fair price. "And you can eat your fill and sleep in the loft above," he said, "where I slept till my blessed mother died."

Soon Danno wondered how he had gotten along without Mary, so tasty was the loaf of bread she baked, so warm the fire she laid before he awoke at dawn, so well scrubbed the hearth when he returned home from the fair or the fields. And he never tired of watching her, slim and quick like a swallow on the wing. Always moving she was, and would never stop cleaning—under things, over things, searching here and there for any stray speck of dirt. Dusting the cupboards, straightening the dresser, pulling the beds away from the walls upstairs and down, folding the linens, washing the washstands! Even the yard she neatened, clearing away broken crockery thrown in a heap behind the house, righting the overturned bucket, cutting back the fern and briars that overtook the garden.

"Come sit beside me and rest yourself," Danno would say, and sometimes Mary did, but more often she would smile and shake her head and keep on with her work. Then she began to clean the cowshed, sweeping away cobwebs in the corners and rummaging about the piles of hay and straw.

"Mary, that's none of your task," protested Danno. "A century of shoveling out the cowshed is no job for a woman as small as yourself.

Besides—now don't be starting on the chicken coop—I have a proposal," and before he knew it himself, Danno was asking her hand in marriage. A look of joy passed over Mary's face, and then a look of sadness, like clouds passing over the mountain.

"Not now," she said. "I cannot marry you now."

"Perhaps, then, with a bit more time?" he asked softly.

She shrugged her shoulders and turned away, scooping up a basket of clothing she'd washed and carrying it out to hang dry on the line. And didn't she gaze over the fields then with a longing that would wring your heart?

After that, Mary began to sicken with something, but though Danno urged her to stay in her loft room and rest, she was never more frantic in her work, cleaning even his own room when he was away, pushing her broom under the settle for the hundredth time, running the rag along every shelf top and rafter by way of a ladder she found in the barn. And from the top of that ladder she fainted and fell and did not get up again. Danno found her and laid her gently on his own bed, placing cool cloths on her face and spooning broth between her lips. It was all for naught. The bloom she had on her faded before his eyes, and Mary died in his arms.

Danno was bereft, but he set about inviting everyone from miles around to Mary's wake. In those days with no funeral parlors about, they laid the body on the kitchen table for three nights before burial, for all to see and share the sorrow—and the food and drink provided by the family. And Danno mourned Mary like one of his own family, make no mistake. He readied the house—there was certainly no need to clean it— and folk from every farm came out of respect for Danno, whom they'd known all his life, whatever they'd not known of Mary. But at twelve o'clock on the first night, there sounded thunderous hoofbeats on the road to his door. In stepped a stranger, pale and dressed in gray, who stormed up to Mary's body and demanded, "Did you find it, or any sign of it?" The roomful of people stood transfixed, and the more so when a voice came from dead Mary's lips, "No, I did not." Then the stranger turned his back and sped away before anyone could move.

Was that the talk of the night and following day? Never had anyone seen or heard the like of it . . . until midnight next, when again the pale rider wrapped in gray stormed Danno's door and shouted at the body, "Did you find it, or any sign of it?"

"No, I did not," answered dead Mary's voice once again. This time, Danno and some of the men went after the stranger, but before they could lay hands on him, he had disappeared into the night, and all they caught was the sound of his horse galloping away.

"What's to be done for Mary to rest in peace?" moaned Danno, and one of his neighbors counseled, "Bring old Mavis," to which all agreed. If anyone understood the ways of the other world, it would be the hermit hag Mavis. Danno was a bit afraid of old Mavis, but for Mary's sake he took himself to her hut, which could have used a good cleaning itself, and begged her to come for the last night of Mary's wake, "to keep the peace and quiet the dead," said Danno.

"Sounds none too quiet now," sniffed Mavis. She muttered and fumed, but in the end she picked up her cane and followed him home by the light of a fading afternoon. Indeed, a full moon rose that night, and with it the sound of a horseman approaching. The room grew quiet as a graveyard. Mavis pushed herself up from the chair with her cane and tottered over to Mary's body, lying there on the kitchen table. In came the pale stranger, strode forward, and demanded, "Did you find it, or any sign of it?"

"No, I did not," answered dead Mary.

Then up spoke Mavis. "By what right," she asked in a forceful voice few recognized, "do you interfere with grieving the dead?"

"I thought no one would ask!" said the stranger. "That woman"—pointing at Mary— "was required to guard the boundaries of our hurling game in the playing fields beyond"— pointing behind the house. "She failed at her work and we lost our golden ball, and there will be no peace in this house till it's found."

Then came a shout from Danno. He seized his mallet and chisel from the corner chest. With heavy strokes, he smashed the mortar from around the niche. He drew out the golden ball and threw it at the pale stranger, who caught it with a practiced hand and turned to dead Mary, saying "Come now, you'll be off with me."

But the hag Mavis signaled the men to close in between him and the door. "This woman is none of your own, but a human changeling," she charged, pointing a long-jointed finger at the stranger, "for she lived here in daylight and fire-light, through many a cockcrow. You have no more command of her. Ask your fairy folk to guard the golden ball."

Mavis waved the glowering stranger away. The men parted to let him go through, the golden ball clutched to his chest, and the last they heard of him was the great horse pelting away in the night. When the assembled company turned toward Mary, she was sitting up with color in her cheeks as bright as the day she first came.

Danno knelt beside her, and Mary looked down at him.

"You asked me a question once," she said. "If you asked it again, I would answer yes." Then the wake became a wedding, where the guests rejoiced in Danno and Mary's happiness, and the old hag Mavis held the place of highest honor.

HAUN+INGS

When the greatest O'Daly bard passed away, they hung his harp on the wall, for who else could make kings weep and queens smile, or sing of heroes' deeds and lost loves as if he had lived them? Surely not I, the bard's last apprentice, who no sooner learned the second half of a song than I forgot the first, or repeated the first and let the second slip away from my mind like water through a sieve. And when I looked up from watching over the bard's last sleep, there was little left to me, for the bard's magical skills had won more glory than gifts and he carried few possessions on the long road from place to place.

It was a great emptiness I felt looking around the cold room where his body lay. In spite of the bard's scorning my meager talents, I had grown attached to him and longed after his power over a banquet of listeners. Soon the women would come to prepare the corpse for burial and collect whatever should go with him on his journey to the next world. The bard's cloak with its silver clasp of sea serpents was sure to be missed if I took it; likewise the bard's bronze-headed staff and his golden ring.

Footsteps tapped on the stone stairs outside the door. There was no time and nothing to claim . . . but there, on the table where the bard had laid it, his old drinking horn, valuable to no one, and who would notice? I snatched it up and thrust it into my threadbare tunic just as the women came keening and weeping to mourn the dead. Whether I stole the bard's drinking horn out of grief or affection or payment or jealousy is hard now to know. I was an orphan chosen more to care for a failing old man than to continue the man's great work. Singers the bard had trained in his prime already harped across the land, and I fell far short of joining them. Whatever was in my heart, I was thrust aside and left to wander away with no place to go and nothing to do, until the gruff chieftain offered me a place as herd boy for the MacCarthy castle, where the bard had ended his days. My only comfort came from a kitchen maid who tied up provisions of oatcake and handed me the packet with a bold wink as I turned to take up my work.

I was accustomed to wandering, and wander I did, though in the company of cows or sheep instead of a human companion. I was also accustomed to keeping silent, the better to listen to the bard, but bellowing and baaing were all I heard now as I moved the cows from field to field or gathered sheep from the mountain heights where they scattered to graze. I swung the drinking horn by its leather thong over my shoulder and used it when I crossed a clear stream, but from the first time I drank out of the horn, strange things began to happen. I not only tasted the cool, sweet water, I was *with* the water—rushing down my own warm throat, rolling in the round drip from my face and splattering to dry on the bushes. I was consuming and consumed, the world magnified inside and out, the sun brighter, the dew more delicate, the winds singing light and dark airs. At first I thought perhaps I was feverish, but I felt well.

It was not long after that when I came upon a glen filled with patches of wispy bog cotton. I should have circled round it, but leaping across from stone to stone would shorten the way. Just in the midst of the bog, my foot slipped and black water squelched around my legs. I began to choke and gasp. Surely I was still standing, but suddenly I felt myself lying tightly bound, water closing over my face . . . my mouth . . . my nose. I struggled to loosen the leather thongs, to breathe. I gagged as the water slipped into my windpipe, filled my lungs. My waterlogged body was sinking . . . hardening . . . flesh encased in peat as seasons passed unfeeling over a sacrifice unmourned.

Yet still I stood, dreaming dead and acting alive at the same time. I shook my head to clear it of these drear hauntings and, throwing myself toward a dry hummock, managed to cross the rest of the bog to hard ground. There I rested awhile and found the trail toward a hilltop that dropped steeply into the sea, a place where the sheep were especially drawn to graze. Moving through a stand of knee-high reeds, I suddenly pitched forward into open space and seemed to split in two again. One of me whirled my arms, caught my balance, and drew back from a deep blowhole through which I caught the hollow sound of pounding surf in the sea cave far below. The other hurtled downward through darkness, crashed onto stones that splintered my bones . . . exhaled bubbles of blood . . . floated out on the tide . . . was torn by mackerel chewing my skin with needley teeth.

I was a scream rising from my own throat, I was backing away as warily as I could from the edge of a death that once claimed another careless herd boy. And what now? Every foot of the land was bathed in the blood of those who came before. "Beware the bones in the bog, beware the stones in the hole below." As the chant came to me, I stood very still, for this was the way I remembered the bard forming a song, first a chant, then a rhythmic cadence with rhymes woven into melody and practiced as we walked the long roads or gazed into a cooking fire under the far stars at night.

I am a wind across the sea,
I am a flood across the plain,

I am the roaring of the tides,
I am a stag of seven tines,
I am a dewdrop drawn by the sun,
I am the fierceness of boars,
I am a hawk, my nest on a cliff,
I am the height of poetry,
I am the fairest among the flowers,
I am the salmon of deepest wisdom.
Who else can be the tree and the lightning
   that strikes it?
Who else, the dark secret of dolmen not yet
   hewn?

I am the queen of every hive,
I am the fire on every hill,
I am the shield over every head,
I am the spear of every fight,
I am the wave of eternal return,
I am the grave of every vain hope.
Who knows the path of the sun, each stage
   of the moon?
Who mends divisions, enthralls the sea,
   and sets
In order the mountains, the rivers, the
   deeds of all people?

* * *

How could I bear this? For the stream and bog
and blowhole were only the start. When next a
thirst came upon me, I found a well and from
it drew water and dipped the bard's drinking
horn into it. No sooner did I take a deep draft
than I was writhing on the ground . . . gored by
a wild boar that ripped open my belly with
curved tusks, blood and pain all over me.
Transformed, I was, into the dying warrior
Dermott O'Duivna, and tricked—as he was—
into a fatal hunt by the greatest warrior, Finn
MacCual. I could hear my comrades begging,
"Bring water from the well, Finn, for the water
cupped in your hands holds healing power."
But Finn MacCual hated me for stealing his
betrothéd Grania. Twice he cupped the well
water in his hands, only to let it slip away. The
third time he came with the water and stood
over me too late, for my wounds were terrible
and my death anguished. They laid a mantle
over me and even the dogs—my hunting
hound and Finn's own Bran—howled long and
loud. Then one of the warriors called out,

Raise the cry for him, gods of stone and moss,
For Dermott with the weapons now
   laid down,
And place him on your green, smooth-sided
   mound,
But we will keep the sorrow of our loss.

A sea of tears fell for the slain hero. Some came
from me as I cried over my own body, but when
I wiped them away, there was only the well of
water beside me and a lonely wind howling
through the valley. I looked down at the drinking
horn in my hand and slowly lifted the leather
thong from off my shoulder. At last I knew what
the bard's secret power had cost, through long
nights of harping, and how unfit were my own
small spikes of envy. So, too, I knew what he most
needed on his last journey to gift the otherworld
with song. I buried the drinking horn that night
beside his grave, under the far stars, and wished
him well for an eternity of singing. And afterward
I found comfort in the company of the bold serv-
ing girl, and was content.

COINS

Angus cherished his wife, Kathleen, but she died and left him with no children to care for, or to care for him. He lived beside a crossroads in a house so small you could stand in the middle and open the front door with one hand and the back door with the other. If you turned around you could reach the kettle and put it on the fireplace to boil water for tea. Behind the house was a garden just as small, with rows of potatoes, cabbages, and onions. In the middle of the garden stood a cherry tree that turned white with blossoms in spring, red with cherries in summer, and dark with blackbirds eating the fruit while rabbits nibbled the garden.

"You'll never have a bite for yourself," said

the neighbors, "unless you drive them away." But Angus laughed and said, "There's enough for all of us," just as Kathleen had done, she of the generous heart.

Angus traveled the countryside with a pack on his back. At every fair and holiday, he'd lay out his wares and there would be a young boy looking at a pennywhistle without a penny to buy it, or a girl longing for a small book of verse when her shawl was too ragged to keep her warm. Often he would draw them aside and whisper, "This will be lighter in your pocket than in my pack." And people said, "When you're old and gray you'll be begging for coins at our door." Still, the dogs in every village followed on his heels, for they knew he'd share his bite of bread and cheese, and the children followed to hear a story, for they knew he'd tell them one, and time passed.

As Angus grew older, his pack grew lighter. So few things were left that it rattled like the hunger in his stomach. Winter came and with it the wind and the rain. Not a coin remained in the peddler's pocket. Not a coin clinked in the jar where Kathleen had saved what she could for hard times. Now hunger is a cruel bedfellow, and it is more than likely that a hungry man will dream. One night as Angus lay sleeping—or dying, he knew not which—he dreamed that Kathleen stood in his doorway and spoke. "Go to Dublin town," she said, "and stand on the bridge over the River Liffey. There you shall hear what you shall hear." Angus called after her, but she faded away, leaving him lonelier than ever before. He woke the next morning troubled in mind, for Dublin was three days' walk away from his village of Ballaghaderreen, and his legs were already weak and trembling with hunger. "I'll stay where I am," he said to the walls, "and rest in peace." The next night, though, came the same dream.

"Go to Dublin town and stand on the bridge over the River Liffey," said the pale shade of his wife, "and you shall hear what you shall hear." Angus had listened well to Kathleen when she was alive and had yearned to hear her voice since she died. Still he stayed where he was. But after the third night and the third dream, he picked up his pack, nearly as empty as his stomach, and set out for Dublin. How he got there it's hard to say, for hunger brings gnawing pain with every step, but get there he did, one weary foot after the other, and found his way to the bridge over the River Liffey. There he stood from dawn to dark, watching people crowd from this side to that or that side to this. At the end of the long day he turned away, thinking he must find a dark alley and die like a dog in the dirt, for he had not the strength to return home. But as Angus moved off the bridge, an innkeeper opened his door and came out to him.

"All day long," said the innkeeper, "I've been watching you stand here like an old crow with raggety wings. And of all the people passing from this side to that or that side to this, not one spoke a word to you. Now I'm curious to know what you're doing here and why, and I'll even feed you to find out." So he led Angus into his inn and gave him bread and cheese and ale. And in return the peddler said, "I came here because I dreamed that I should come."

"A dream." The innkeeper laughed. "You came here to follow a dream?"

"Do you not dream yourself?" asked Angus.

"The dream I follow is the sound of coins in

my pocket," said the innkeeper as he showed Angus to the door. But then he stopped. "I did have a dream." He smiled. "Three nights running. I dreamed that a woman as poor as yourself came to this very door and pointed to the road running westward. 'Go to Ballaghaderreen,' she said, and 'There beside the crossroads you'll find a small house, and behind the small house a garden, and in the garden a cherry tree. Dig beneath that tree and you'll find gold, much gold.'" The innkeeper rattled the coins in his pocket again. "Ballaghaderreen," he said, and shook his head. "A likely story."

"Ah," said Angus, "perhaps it is," and he turned and started the long walk home. How he got there it's hard to say but get there he did, one weary foot after the other, and went directly to his little garden with a spade in his hand. Then he dug under the cherry tree, and dug and dug until he felt a hard thud. Brushing away the dirt, he uncovered an old chest, curiously designed, and opened it to find clumps of gold coins musty and molded together with mildew—pieces of eight and Spanish doubloons.

Angus was as generous with that gold as he

had been without it, giving as well as spending, and telling the story with it. His small house by the crossroads became a resting place for all weary travelers going from here to there and there to here. After he died, he was laid in his own resting place beside his beloved wife, Kathleen, and wild ivy joined their graves. As to the neighbors, they quickly spent the golden coins he had left them, but they kept his story forever.

Nurse's Fee

Jane Kingston lived alone. Her cottage looked out over the Bay of Gales, so named for the ferocious crosscurrents of wind that whipped the coast on stormy days. Many a ship had gone down at sea while racing to beat a storm into the bay, but the bay was filled with hidden rocks where breakers could sink a laden vessel.

The land surrounding Jane's cottage held secrets of its own. From the gate of her wild, walled garden snaked a sunken pathway overhung with tangled branches. Anyone could pass along it without being seen from the nearby fields. This leafy tunnel emerged in a graveyard near the ruins of an ancient church, its Celtic crosses marked with mysterious symbols half erased by centuries of rain. There was rumored to be an underground passage leading from beneath one of the gravestones down to a watery cavern accessible to small boats and convenient for smuggling unidentified goods or persons.

Jane paid no attention to such stories. She was a sensible sort, content to tend her garden, her cow, her collie, and her cat. Shc had planned to see the world when her mother died after years of Jane's attending her through bitter illness. Somehow the day never came for Jane to leave, though she was still young and could always set out. Jane remained a mystery to the villagers, an outsider not by birth but by habit. She lived on a small allowance passed down in dwindling amounts, first to her mother and now to her, from an unmarried great-uncle enriched by merchandizing of one kind and another— some said smuggling. He had kept the seaside cottage as a retreat from the social demands of the city, but for Jane it provided, year in and year out, a society of its own, including not only her animals but also a cove of gray seals in the sea below and clouds of birds above. She gave bread crumbs to the birds and sometimes threw a few of the mackerel she had caught to the seals, who did not mind a mouthful of bony fish. She did this in the evening when no one was about. Fishermen competed with seals for their catch and ran over them with whirling propellers or shot them if they neared the nets. Occasionally, a scarred carcass washed onto the stony beach. Then the place would stink until time and tide picked the bones clean.

The day Jane found the injured seal was wintry and overcast. The sky matched the seal, a soft, thick gray, but its fur was streaked with blood. The propeller had dug deep, and the big seal lay on one side. At first Jane thought it was dead, but when she leaned near, it opened eyes deep with pleading. When the seal moved, Jane's collie, Cap, jumped back and began to bark.

"Hush, Cap, the beast is hurt," said Jane. She lowered her hand, and the collie lowered his black-and-white body to the ground, waiting. Jane touched the seal, and it groaned like a human. When she glanced out to sea, a head rose in the water, watching. Its mate, thought

Jane. The seal mate, its arched nose pointing toward her, waited without moving in the water. Cap waited without moving on the land. Jane did not know what to do. "I'm no nurse," she whispered to the seal. And then she heard a whimper from behind a rock nearby. The seal struggled to move but could not. Even as Jane watched, its breathing stopped and its eyes trailed death into the distance.

The whimpering continued. Jane followed the sound and found what she half expected, a white seal pup recently born, perhaps three feet long, about the weight of her own dog, Cap. She knew the way of the wild. Orphaned babies die. The seal is a wild animal. Not to take home. And then the pup whimpered again and surrounded her with its sad, hungry eyes. She took off her raincoat and rolled the seal pup onto it, wrapping him round and heaving him up in her arms. Cap followed close on her heels as she picked her way around the rocks toward the wild, walled garden.

The next days consisted of thin oatmeal porridge, thick cream, and fish, all mashed together and watered down enough to feed the pup from an oilskin bag tied tightly around the tube of an old funnel. At first Jane squeezed the bag, forcing the mixture into the tube and down the pup's throat, but he soon began to suck on the tube himself, every few hours, dawn till dark. Gone were Jane's hours of reading. She caught messes of mackerel from her skiff, always careful to steer clear of the infamous rocks that guarded her shore. Her precious silence was interrupted by the endless whining of the hungry pup and by the work of preparing his next meal, washing him down in the old cowshed, and feeding him once again. Jane was steeped in the smell of fish. Cap watched, the cat circled, the cow gave creamy milk.

After a week, Jane forced a whole fish far enough down the pup's throat to make him swallow, and then he was eating the fish eagerly of his own accord. As soon as she could, Jane would return the pup to shore, where he could venture into the sea, catch his own food, and rejoin his seal kin. The pup gained weight quickly. His long white baby coat began to molt, leaving short fur that was gray with a darker pattern like clouds chasing across a stormy sky.

Already he hitched himself along the ground after her, but she waved her arms and shouted at him not to follow. Following humans to find fish had killed his mother.

"Tomorrow, Greedy-Guts, you will go home," she said one evening as she left him for the night. Then she went inside to bathe away the smell of fish and feed herself. The cat was nowhere to be seen. Jane found her hidden in the closet, a sure sign of bad weather. Cap was restless. He paced the floor, barking at the door till Jane finally let him out. Then in again and out again and in. Finally she followed him into the garden and found him herding the seal pup toward the house, nudging and circling, nudging and circling till it hitched itself to the back door. Jane read the sky and read the dog. "Aye, then," she said, "there's a big storm brewing," and she shut the cow into the shed and the seal pup inside the front mudroom with the boots and coats to settle down for the night. Still Cap whined and paced the house till she shut him, too, into the mudroom so she could rest in peace. The two animals would keep each other company.

BETSY HEARNE

The wind picked up around midnight, heralding one of the wild gales for which the bay was named. Jane woke suddenly from heavy sleep. What had startled her? She was used to the wind, the wind's howling . . . but not to the sound of steps dragging along her floor toward the bedroom door. For a moment she wondered if somehow the pup had opened her door, but when she turned to rise, she found herself looking up into the eyes of a man. He was naked, thickly muscled yet shivering. Water dripped from his dark hair, around his black eyes, down the strong nose and flat planes of his face. He seemed bewildered and looked about the room as if he were the one surprised and not she.

Jane pulled the blanket around her and stood up.

"Who are you?" she asked. "What is it you want?"

Slowly the man turned his gaze toward her and spoke with effort. "My son," he said. "Give to me my little young son." She knew those words, *give to me my little young son*. Somewhere from an old song. She was dreaming a song, from nights in a rocking chair when her mother crooned her to sleep. The words swam up from deep memory.

> An earthly nurse sits and sings
> And, aye, she sings, ba lilly wean
> Little ken I my bairn's father
> Far less the land that he stays in.

> Then in steps he to her bed fit,
> And a grumley guest I'm sure was he;
> Saying, Here I am, thy bairn's father
> Although I be not comely.

The man stood before her unmoving, and the song streamed through her mind.

> I am a man upon the land,
> I am a selkie in the sea
> And when I'm far and far from land
> My home it is in Sule Skerry.

> Then he has taken a purse of gold,
> And he has put it upon her knee
> Saying, give to me my little young son
> And take thee up thy nurse's fee.

It shall come to pass on a summer's day,
When the sun shines hot on every stone,
That I shall take my little young son
And teach him for to swim the foam.

How odd to hear singing in a dream, to be dreaming that she had awakened. Jane almost laughed with relief. Caring for the seal pup had made her dream of selkies. She was dreaming still. Water pooled on her floor and the stranger shivered. He made no threatening move, so at last she took pity on him and threw the blanket around his shoulders and led him into the kitchen. When Jane lit the fire, he backed away in fear. She took his hand and pulled him toward it, into the chair where she read her books. His fingers were long and tapering and partially webbed. He would not stay in the chair but rolled himself into the blanket on the rug and stared hypnotized at the flames. She brewed sweet tea and made him drink it. "In the morning," she said, "in the morning I will give to thee thy little young son."

Then he drew his gaze from the fire and

covered her with his eyes. She lay down beside him, still dreaming, surely dreaming, and dreamed a night that few could imagine and fewer still remember. The dream rose and receded and rose again in tidal waves, wet and warm, slippery cool, coral sparks circled in blue, a suspended space of water and fire sliding together.

Yet there was snarling at the end of the dream, and wild cries.

Sunlight woke her, the first morning she had slept past dawn since caring for the pup. She was alarmed to find herself rolled in a blanket by the cold fire. She must have sleepwalked in her dream. She could hear no sound, no wind, no seal pup whimpering, no dog whining. Jane dressed and opened the mudroom door. The hallway stood empty except for coats and boots collapsed on the floor in a jumble. She strode from the front of the house to the kitchen, almost tripping over a heavy leather pouch that lay in her way. The back door hung open. Outside, Cap staggered about the garden, blood matted on his head, stopping to paw at the garden gate and return to her with hurt but urgent eyes. She knelt beside him and ran her hands over his body. His legs and torso were sound—only there on the head, a great lump on his head. He pulled away from her and back to the garden gate.

Jane followed him, wondering, into the wet new world and opened the back gate. Nose to the ground, Cap tracked through the green tunnel that led to the graveyard. Jane followed him with her arms held out against the overgrown branches. When they came to the graveyard, Cap charged toward one of the large gravestones, which at first glance seemed to have fallen over in the storm. As Jane drew closer she saw a hole beside it with steps leading into the ground. Already Cap had disappeared into it. Slowly Jane let herself down into the hole, feeling her way from step to step, stooping then straightening as the tunnel leveled and opened up. From somewhere ahead came a faint light and the crash of waves. Suddenly the tunnel sloped downward and opened onto a great space. The sea cavern loomed toward a stony-toothed mouth that at low tide could allow a knowing rowboat in and out but at high tide would close. Under her feet was a hidden pebble beach, and before her in the water bobbed two heads, one large and one small, watching. Then they disappeared under the water with a flippered wave, and Jane was left remembering a dream, or dreaming of a memory.

Whichever it was, she never married. The gold in the old leather pouch supplied her well, and she knew the end of the song and would not let it happen.

And thou shalt marry a proud gunner,
And a proud gunner I'm sure he'll be
And the very first shot that ever he'll shoot
He'll kill both my young son and me.

+HE CROSSING

Here is a story short to tell but long to end.

Brown-haired Meg MacDermott loved her sister, Una, but she adored her sister's secret sweetheart. Thomas was strong, Thomas was bold, and Thomas was handsome. He could win at any game and win any girl's heart, but red-haired Una had claimed him, she with the green eyes and smile that flashed like silver light on black water.

Meg and Una were two years apart and the pride of their father, yet Connor MacDermott was a stiff man, given more to hard work than affection, and once formed, his likes and dislikes never changed. Alas, he disliked Una's sweetheart and forbade Thomas to court her, for Thomas was not of their people, and Una's father nursed bitter grievance against those of a different church or lineage. So it was that Meg became the lovers' messenger and felt honored by the task.

It was not easy for Una and Thomas to meet, since Connor MacDermott was out and about the farm, keeping his eye on everything that had to be done. His wife always bent to her husband's will, cruel or otherwise, and Meg and Una watched this with dread for their own futures.

Thomas was freer to roam. His father had been an officer who left his mother a rich widow with a house in town the envy of her neighbors. She doted on Thomas and longed to keep him home from the wars that killed his father. To make it so, she gave him all he wanted, and it's a wonder he grew up unspoiled, though he could be impetuous and willful. The harder it was to see Una, the more he pressed to see her— an embrace against a willow tree beside the lake, a long kiss behind mossy crosses in the Church of England graveyard (where none of her people would be caught dead), a quick word or two while she ran errands, and many a meeting of eyes whenever chance or planning brought them together. And no meeting could take place without a message carried by Meg.

"Tell Thomas, midnight at the rath," Una would whisper to Meg, who would manage to slip away on some pretext and find Thomas. Or Thomas would stop Meg on the way home from market.

"Tell Una I'll wait by the holy well when she comes back from early mass." And Thomas would slip Meg a silver coin, though Meg was just as happy with a pat on the back from her idol.

As often as not, it was letters that Meg carried, letters declaring Una's love for Thomas and his for her. Meg swore an oath to both, never to read or reveal them, but she knew where Una kept hers, hidden away in an old leather pouch wedged under two broken standing stones.

Connor MacDermott grew suspicious, for Una would receive no other suitor. One day he entered agreement with a farmer, much like himself, though younger, who lived not far away and coveted Una as well as the fine dowry promised with her. Una wept, Thomas raged, and they began to arrange their escape. Thomas would draw on his inheritance, they would go to the city, board a ship, and make the crossing to America. Meg carried their last letters— Thomas's instructions and Una's pledge—but this time Meg was not so lucky at dodging her father, who caught and beat her black and blue, read the letters, and hired a boat to take Una across the lake to an island convent.

"And there you can stay, lass, till you learn not to cross your father."

Stay she did, but stopped eating as well, till her bones grew brittle and her pale skin so thin you could see the blue veins beneath. Nearly transparent she was when she died. Meg carried that message to Thomas, as well, and saw him go wild with grief, run to the lake shore, and leap into the water, saw him swim straight for the island, farther, farther, farther, strong strokes at first, then slower, slower. No man survived this crossing— the lake was said to swallow those who defied it. Meg watched heartstruck as Thomas's head bobbed a last time, then disappeared.

They found his body next day, and before the year was out, Meg had run away herself, booked passage to America with the money saved from messages carried, and boarded ship for the crossing. She left behind her a packet of crumbling letters, two dead lovers, two grieving mothers, and a father guarded by day against regrets but beset by dreams, at night, of his lost children.

That is the short of it.

The long of it is Meg surviving the Atlantic voyage, finding work and a husband in America, and begetting children who followed, in turn, their own ways. It is a story not without sadness, but offering some measure of choice. So may it be in our time, and yours.

✝HE LE✝✝ER

May 5, 1851

Dear Grandpapa,

I take pen in hand at the request of Mama to give you the sad news that we have been struck by misfortune. It is hard to believe that we came through so much—the drought, the insects, the sickness, the stillbirth of baby Ben—only to have all we worked for destroyed by a twisting wind. Like the wrath of God, it took the cabin, the barn with all the livestock, and the crop that we had counted on to pay back what Papa borrowed on the farm. Even more strange is that none of our neighbors' property was touched.

We are indeed lucky to be alive, though Papa is not well. Mama saw the wind coming afar off—twirling, as she said later, like a snake from the sky to the ground—and made us all go down to the root cellar. Papa would not go but was determined to secure the barn door. When we came up, there was nothing left except broken logs and uprooted trees and dead or dying animals. Papa lay unconscious with a terrible head wound that affects his ability to speak or move freely.

Only one thing still stood, perfectly preserved—the wagon on which we loaded our goods to come here with great expectations so long ago. Then we realized, upon looking more closely, that the wagon had been picked up and turned around like a toy, pointing East instead of West. Mama takes it as a sign to return home to you in Philadelphia, along with Papa, Toby, and Melissa. I will stay here in Ohio, as I am sixteen now and engaged to be married to Elijah Smith, the son of our good Dr. Smith, who is caring for Papa. I earn a bit by writing letters and assisting the teacher with her younger pupils, and Mama has given permission to set the wedding date earlier than we planned, before they leave.

I must confess myself torn. When Elijah and

I pass the old wagon on our Sunday walks, it seems to stare sadly at the sky, empty of all our hopes and dreams. I suppose we must ever turn to new ones, yet I am sometimes drawn back to the wagon, as if against my will, and wonder what the future holds.

We trust this letter finds you and Grandmama in good health and that you will anticipate a reunion with your daughter and family before long.

Ever with respect and affection, etc., from your dutiful granddaughter,

Leora

PART II
THE PRESENT
(SET MOSTLY IN THE UNITED STATES)

FALL

Nell climbs the folding trapdoor stairs and looks around. She has not been up here for a long time. The wooden chest stands between a folded crib and an old-fashioned, big-wheeled buggy. Her old toy crow sits propped against a pair of roller skates on top of the chest. She picks him up, a black rag doll with jet-button eyes, yellow beak, long yellow legs, a blue-checked bandanna, overalls, and a straw hat. Now that she knows the ways of the world, she sees the irony of a crow dressed like a scarecrow—something to scare itself away. Light slips in the window and slides a finger over the dusty corners of the attic.

Leaning beside the crow is a tattered book of

nursery rhymes. Nell strokes the crow's beak. *One for sorrow, two for joy, three for girls, and four for boys, five for silver, six for gold, seven for a secret never to be told.* The crow seems to stir in her hands. People think nursery rhymes are for children, but Nell knows they are messages. In code. About death.

There was an old woman tossed in a blanket
Seventeen times as high as the moon;
But where she was going no mortal could tell,
For under her arm she carried a broom.
"Old woman, old woman, old woman," said I,
"Whither, ah whither, ah whither so high?"
"To sweep the cobwebs from the sky,
And I'll be with you by and by."

The wail of a train drifts toward her. Nell goes to the window and looks over the fields. Faraway freight cars snake by like George's model railroad set, long abandoned in the attic. Her brother has not played with anything for a long time. She can see him driving the harvester back and forth in a globe of corn dust. Her father, who could be her brother's twin but for the years between them, drives the tractor back to the barn. Nearby the garden droops. A few tomatoes bleed off the vines and pumpkins glow on the ground, but frost has killed everything else.

Under some old maples—their leaves sifting the October sun with a gold and crimson screen—she can see the stone marking Bell's grave. Bell is a noisy name, but Bell is not noisy. Bell is forever silent. Little Bell, always newborn. If she saw Bell now, Nell would be able to see herself as a baby. But she does not want to see Bell now, the little bones, the little earthen body. Better to leave her alone in the loam. There lies Bell, here sits Nell, twins parted by time.

A shadow crosses the floorboards, and a gray muzzle rests on her lap. Nell looks down at the dog, exactly her own age but old now—a mean trick of nature. Her brother George found him abandoned in a trick-or-treat bag. The doorbell rang, but no one was there, just a black paper bag with yellow jack-o'-lantern stickers on it and a brown puppy inside. It was the same Halloween night Nell and Bell were born, so George named the puppy Dell. Nell, Bell, Dell.

The farmer in the dell, the farmer in the dell, hi, ho, the dairy-oh, the farmer in the dell . . . That's Dell's song.

Bell has a song, too. *Are you sleeping, are you sleeping* . . . *Morning bells are ringing, morning bells are ringing, Din dan don.* That's Bell's song, only she never wakes up to hear it.

"Nell?" calls her father from somewhere down below. "Nell, where are you?"

Quickly she puts the crow on the toy chest and backs down the treacherous trapdoor stairs, nose to nose with Dell, who walks down frontways slowly and carefully after her. She folds the stairs and trapdoor back toward the ceiling and calls out, "Here, Dad, just cleaning my room." Today is Friday, her short day at school. She has chores.

"It's time to start dinner. Your brother's doing a hard day's work."

As Nell steps downstairs toward the kitchen, silence settles in the attic. She knows what will happen next—a faint sound, the clack of a beak and a strangled *caw*. The toy crow will flap its black cotton wings, hop a few steps on its long yellow legs, and flutter toward the window, beating against the glass as if its heart will shatter.

Nell can't remember exactly when she realized the crow was alive. She does remember finding it. Her mother had just gone away. They were still hoping then that she would come back. Her father drove them to town for groceries and library books. It was fall, then, too. She was six years old but already a good reader. Nell got her books and wandered toward the truck, past porches with carved pumpkin faces leering at passersby. She was a little scared and very, very lonely. Sitting beside the curb, waiting for pickup, was a box of old junk—and on top of the box of old junk was the scary scarecrow-crow, waiting for her. She picked him up to see if he was too raggedy to take home. He stared back at her with beady eyes, no dirt or holes anywhere on his sponge-stuffed body. She wondered who had thrown him out, and why. But it didn't matter. He could keep her company.

For some reason she hid him under her jacket, maybe to stave off her brother's teasing. It wasn't till later, after she had put him upstairs in the attic, that she began to hear the noises of his flapping and banging against the window. She has been hearing it for a long time, seven years.

She is in and out of time now, slipping between the pile of dirty dishes that she should have done earlier, and yet she's flapping with the crow against the window, desperate to fly outside and away from the house. A glass slips from her hands and crashes against a plate, shattering into jagged pieces. Nell begins to cry just as her brother barges through the back door stomping mud off his work boots.

"What's wrong?" he yells at her. "What happened?"

She points to broken glass. It's mounded with rainbow-colored soap bubbles.

"Oh, for Pete's sake," he says. "I thought . . . come on, Nell, stop it. You're a mess. The whole place is a mess. I thought you were supposed to clean up the house today." He hangs up his jacket on its wooden peg. "What's for dinner?"

Nell sniffles in reply and begins cleaning up the broken glass.

"Nothing, as usual," he says. "All afternoon I've been in the field, you haven't done a thing." He turns his back on her and storms up the stairs.

Her father opens the back door, takes one look around, shakes his head, and passes behind her toward the TV in the living room. She hears the shower upstairs, the news blaring nearby, and the crow shrieking from the attic. Nell dumps the broken glass into the garbage and dries her hands. Then she leaves the house and heads toward the trees. Beside the gravestone, she kneels in the damp leaves. "Bell," she whispers, "come back. I need you." She does not know how much time has passed, but it's dark before her brother comes out and finds her. He wraps her in his jacket and leads her back into the house.

Nell goes to bed and falls deep asleep. When she wakes up, the whole house is silent as a held breath. She gets out of bed and goes to the bathroom. She almost trips over Dell, who is too deaf to hear her coming and too brown to show up in the dark. Her father's door and her brother's door are closed. Back in her room, she pulls the blankets around her into a nest. The nights are getting cold. She's staring up at the ceiling when the noises start again, the flapping, the cawing. She closes her eyes for a minute, and when she opens them again, there stands Bell. Surprisingly, Bell is not a skeletal baby with bits of cloth hanging from her bones. She is Nell's age. Well, they are, after all, twins. Time may be no different in the world of the dead. Bell is crying, Nell can tell because she glows faintly—just enough to be clearly visible—and the tears look like ice beads sliding down her face. Bell reaches out, and Nell can feel the touch of a cool hand. Nell tries to hold the hand, but her fingers close on themselves. She is only holding her own hand. Now Nell begins to cry, too, and Bell fades away, drifting toward the ceiling, disappearing through the closed trapdoor. As she goes, her face falls so that she looks old. "Don't go," cries Nell. "Please don't leave."

Frantically Nell leaps from the bed, pulls down the trapdoor, unfolds and climbs the narrow stairs. The attic is a black hole, without sound or glow of ghostly light. Nell feels a lead weight of tiredness pulling her backwards. If she doesn't grip the worn wood, she will fall. She climbs down and gets into bed without bothering to fold the stairs up and close the trapdoor. She is too tired. Yet the nest of blankets now seems to strangle her. The more she twists and turns, the tighter and hotter they feel. Finally she gets up and drags a blanket over to Dell, still sleeping soundly on the rug beside her desk. He lifts his head when he feels her curl up next to him and lays his soft chin on the arm she wraps around him. Then they both sleep.

Next morning the smell of coffee and bacon wakes her. She dresses and slips downstairs, stopping just by the kitchen door. She can sense they are talking about her, like Dell can scent rabbits. The air smells of arguing.

"I swear she's getting worse," says George. He says it in a tired way, like he's repeating the same thing for the tenth time but doesn't know any other way to say it.

"She's a teenager. She's just acting out," says her father.

"Dad, I never went through anything like this."

"She's a girl."

"It's not just that. I think she needs help."

"Let me worry about it. You go on and get to work now."

Her father rattles the *Farmer's Weekly*, and George closes his face and grabs his jeans jacket on the way out the door. Nell waits for a few minutes till her father stands up with his empty coffee cup and clinks it down beside the sink. She peeks around the corner. No one has done the dishes. Last night's and this morning's have piled up beside those she hadn't finished when the glass broke. Her father scribbles a note and strides out the door after her brother. When they are both out of sight, she enters the kitchen and reads the note. DO THE DISHES. Saturday stretches before her. The days of the week do not matter to farm work; only the weather matters. If it is time to harvest, Saturdays and Sundays are just like Mondays. But unlike her father and brother, she will go to school on Monday, if she can just get through Saturday and Sunday.

Tonight there is a dance at school. She will not go because no one has invited her. She has watched at lunchtime, though, while they decorate the gym—twisty orange and black crepe ribbons draped across the ceiling, a fake paper moon, corny cardboard spiders hung from wisps of angel-hair web. There will be dry-ice fog and creepy music. She doesn't even want to go.

Besides, it's her birthday. Number thirteen. She wonders if there will be any trick-or-treaters coming this far out into the country. Too bad if they come—she forgot to get candy. She wonders who left Dell at their door that Halloween night and if they knew what a good dog he'd be. If only Bell had lived, too. Everything would be different if Bell were here. Nell has said this to herself so many times it has worn a pathway through her brain cells. She can imagine Bell and herself going to the dance together, doing the dishes together, whispering down the halls of school, playing tricks on George, taking walks with Dell.

Maybe she will take a walk with old Dell, now that she has finally finished the dishes. Soon there will be lunch dishes to do. It would be so much easier not to eat. Nell dries her hands and goes looking—Dell can't hear her calling anymore. He's not downstairs, but probably up in her room, that's where he stays most of the time now.

Her room is empty. Nell glances up the folding stairs through the open trapdoor. She should have closed it last night. Could he be in the attic? Slowly she climbs up the trapdoor stairs. Yes, Dell is there. Like a good dog, he has gone where he can be alone, in the farthest corner of the house, to die.

At first Nell thinks he is just asleep. She touches him, but he does not raise his head—for the first time ever. She sees that he is not breathing, and the air presses down on her so she can barely breathe herself. She hears a muffled sound behind her. The crow is starting again. She can't bear it, cannot stand to hear the cawing and flapping at the window anymore. Nell grabs the crow and struggles to open the window with her other hand, but it won't budge.

"Remember the broken glass?" whispers Bell. "Break the glass." Nell cannot see Bell, but she can hear her clearly. Nell grabs one of her old skates and crashes it through the window, over and over again. When the glass is mostly gone, she flings the crow as far as she can. "Fly!" she screams. "Fly away home!" Nell watches the toy hurtle in an arc toward the gravestone. *There were two blackbirds sat upon a stone, one flew away and then there was one. The other flew after and then there was none.* Nell climbs up on the glass-filled windowsill, looks back once at Dell's body, holds her arms out, and falls.

She can hear someone calling her, first far away, then near. "My God, girl, what have you done?" She is lying on her back with one leg twisted and bloody. There is a bone sticking through the skin. Her father sounds angry. What has she done?

"Dell died," she whispers.

"When, where?"

"In the attic. Dell died, and I'm the only one left."

"What do you mean? What happened?"

"Bell and Dell. And Mama. They're all gone, and now me, I'm next." Her leg hurts so much.

"Dell was old. Bell died getting born. Your mother's long gone, wherever she went off to, and you may look like her—you may even act like her on a bad day—but by God, you're not going anywhere. Now don't move. I have to call the doctor."

Nell is afraid to move. Not just her leg hurts, but everything else, her head, her heart. Everything hurts. She can't bear it. She can't bear being left behind again. But her father is gone, and she hears Bell whisper.

There was an old woman tossed in a blanket
Seventeen times as high as the moon;
But where she was going no mortal could tell,
For under her arm she carried a broom.
"Old woman, old woman, old woman," said I,
"Whither, ah whither, ah whither so high?"
"To sweep the cobwebs from the sky,
And I'll be with you by and by."

LOOSE
CHIPPINGS

My mother can't fly without tranquilizers. She swallowed one before we got on the plane and another as we buckled our seat belts.

"Lucas, you're being hyperactive." Mom closed her eyes and breathed deeply, part of her meditation routine. I tried to figure out which part of my body had moved. The five of us were lined up like a fire drill. Dad on the aisle seat, impatient to get going. My older sister, Julie, calm and beautiful and smart and on her way to spend a semester in London. Me. My other sister, angel baby Megan. My mother, trying to unclench her fists, where each white knuckle strained the skin of her thin hands.

Julie leaned forward. "Stop flailing around,

Lucas." College students use words like flailing. Then she whispered past me, "Just seven hours, Mom." My mother smiled at her with tears nearly sliding from the sides of her eyes. Megan kept reading *Lord of the Rings*, which is much too old for her, like all our lives depended on wizard magic. I stared at soothing pictures of clouds and waterfalls flickering across the screen at the front of the cabin and listened to the elevator music piped through the headphones that our attendant had just handed out. Then the engines revved, the land slipped away under us, and we bet our lives on the little engines bearing us three thousand miles across air and ocean.

Dad, Julie, Megan, and finally Mom slept. I twitched, trying to find comfortable corners for my bony body. They don't give tranquilizers to average teenage males for average transatlantic flights. At least, we all hoped it would be average, though by the time the plane thumped down on the wet runway at Heathrow Airport, I had died a lot of times by fire and water in nonstop disaster fantasies. Who needs villains like Sauron when you can torment yourself?

The train ride into London was a blur of

swaying passengers and bumping bags. For a family of five, just one bag each is still five bags. We took up more than our share of space in a packed compartment. Megan played peek-a-boo with a little boy across the aisle. Julie stared expectantly out the window. Mom and Dad coped. I closed my gritty eyes and finally began to doze just as Dad nudged us to get ready for the next stop. By the time we checked into the hotel, I wanted more than anything else in the world just to take a nap in the cold white sheets of the folding cot. Our budget allowed for only one hotel room, so it was going to be a cozy vacation. Mom and Dad claimed one double bed and Julie would double up in the other with Megan.

Unfortunately, warm little Megan—fresh from hours of sound sleep—wanted nothing more than to see Buckingham Palace right away because that is where, she said, the BFG had crawled through the window into the Queen of England's bedroom. And equally fresh Julie, it turned out, had an interest in red-uniformed young men in tall furry hats. So, both of them strained to catch sight of (1) a big ugly giant hiding in the bushes below the palace windows, or (2) a big handsome guard smitten by the sudden appearance of an American college girl. I dragged myself far enough behind them to inflict some guilt for my suffering.

The changing of the guard was, in my father's words, a sight for sore eyes—an expression I could relate to now that my eyes were actually sore. But then Megan slipped her hand into mine and looked up at me with her own eyes shining like the sky.

"Remember our little tin soldiers, Lucas?"

The tin soldiers lined up in my mind—a miniature army of the ones right in front of us. I had moved my tin soldiers around but never imagined how they'd really look alive, marching with arms and legs raised and lowered stiffly like machines, like some giant was playing with human soldiers. I used to set mine up and knock them over with toy cannons or charge into them with little cast-iron cavalry horses. Sometimes my father brought home toy tanks or airplanes from a business trip, to update the battles. Megan always begged me to let her play, and I did, sometimes. It was embarrassing to play war games with your kid sister, but she had some kind of power over me. Maybe it was her total lack of meanness.

By the time we had strolled from Buckingham Palace through Green Park and set out along the streets toward our hotel, it was getting dark. Our London Plan began with an early cheap dinner, a good night's sleep, some sightseeing next day, and afterward a fancy Soho restaurant that Mom and Dad had read about and saved up for, a real splurge. Dad had studied the map and knew where to go. He was holding Megan's hand, with Mom and Julie following behind and me trailing along like a zombie. Even so, I noticed this weird thing. There was a car parked alongside the curb, a black car, and a guy in black was crouching behind the open door, staring down the block toward a big building. He was kind of hunkered down in the gutter with his back toward us and something held up in his hands, like a little camera maybe. A woman was huddled down over the right-hand steering wheel inside. She was wearing black, too, and she looked up just as I passed by—looked right at me. It was getting dark, but the streetlights were on. Her face looked tense and dead white against all that black. I turned to look back at the guy and wondered if maybe they needed help or if they were filming a movie or something. A little way past them, my father stopped.

"Hey, there's Liberty's," he said, pointing just ahead. "It's a famous department store."

Then I got hit by the sound, like a tsunami. A white flash lit up the street ahead, and I saw my dad the ex-Marine throw Mom and the girls against a building with his body covering them. He was yelling, "Lucas, get down, get down," and I dived after them. All the rest of us were crying-scared, and we could hear screams up ahead. Mom covered Megan's eyes so she wouldn't see. I looked. Flames showed people crumpled on the ground and other people running over to them. Glass was broken all over the blood-pooled sidewalk. A woman's leg lay yards away from her. My dad gathered us up and pushed us in the other direction. I noticed, as we rushed along, that the black car was gone.

When we got back to the hotel my dad turned on the BBC and we heard the same screaming over and over again. The strange thing was that you could see the whole thing more clearly on TV. A camera crew had already filmed the building on fire and interviewed some of the victims crying into a microphone. How does it feel to get blown up? And I kept thinking, just a few more steps and I could have been crying into that microphone, trying to answer stupid questions about how it feels to get blown up. Nobody knew who did it, or why, some kind of terrorists making a political point about British policy. The authorities were asking for witnesses to come forward. There were pictures of the police combing the streets, but there were no pictures of the car and the guy in black crouching beside it and the woman huddled over the steering wheel and I started thinking about that.

"Dad?" I said, and I told him what I had seen. Dad got on the phone to the front desk, and soon I was down in the lobby staring at a guy in a raincoat who looked like every guy I had ever seen. Dan something. He was from Scotland Yard, but no pipe or Sherlock Holmes hat or anything, just very businesslike. I told him three times how we had passed this car parked by the curb but it looked weird, with a man in black crouched behind an open door and a woman huddled behind the steering wheel. After he tested me on the details a couple of times, he asked if I could identify the man and woman. I said probably the woman, maybe the man though I just saw him from the side. Then he asked my dad a lot of questions, like why are you in London? (We're here for a week to drop our oldest daughter off for a semester abroad. Then we'll be vacationing in Ireland.) Why are you going to Ireland? (We are taking a vacation there.) What do you plan to do in Ireland? (We are just taking a vacation there.) Why Ireland? (We're tracing some old family ties there.) What family ties, where? (A graveyard in County Cork.) How long will you be staying here in London? (A week.) Could you stay longer if we need to contact you? (That would be difficult.) Where can we contact you in Ireland? (We will be in County Cork and traveling along the west coast.) Do you have an address where we can reach you? (Yes, I can give you that information.) And back in the U.S., where can we reach you there?

It was hard to tell whether he thought we

were dangerous or in danger. My eyes were blurring and my thoughts floating like clouds past the window of an airplane. Our flight seemed like a century ago. I remember my dad steering me back up to the hotel room and into my cot and then a gray blank till near lunchtime the next day. I woke up with Megan staring down at me with her blue eyes about two inches from my own. Julie was frantically filing her nails and fuming about how she might be late to her appointment, scheduled two hours later, to see the place where she'd be staying for fall semester. Go figure.

Mom treated us all to tea and scones, and Dad said we needed to start over and try to have a good time on our vacation. My parents are big on making the best of things. There was nothing we could do about what had happened except to get on with our plans. I wasn't so sure about that. What if Dan the detective tracked down somebody suspicious and asked me to identify the couple I saw? That part seemed easy, but there was something scary about it, too, like a two-edged sword, as my dad would say. If I could identify them, they could also identify me.

If the couple in the black car was involved, that woman got a clear shot of my face, like she was memorizing me, and she'd know I was a witness. If you're comfortable hurting a random stranger or two just to make a point, wouldn't it be even easier to target someone who could expose you as a criminal? I could be a threat. I could be dead meat. But like Dad said, what could I do about it, anyway, except keep it to myself so as not to worry the rest of the family, and watch every suspicious stranger on the street. There were a lot of them.

Mom and Dad did seem pretty determined to keep us moving so there'd be no time to brood. In the next couple of days we did it all: Madame Tussaud's Wax Museum, the British Museum, the Bethnal Green Museum of Childhood (full of tin soldiers), the Tower of London, Hyde Park, and Julie's damp apartment, called a flat, and was it ever flat, in a crowded neighborhood where we ate fish and chips and planned our tour of Kew Gardens. Whenever we could, we got seats on top of the double-decker buses so we could see the sights. The only thing was, we didn't get to the fancy restaurant right away. At first, Megan didn't feel like eating. Then she started whining about a stomachache. Personally, I think she was upset, but finally, on our next-to-last day, Mom and Dad decided she was just worn-out, and they called the front desk for a baby-sitter to stay with her in the hotel while the rest of us went off to the restaurant. There weren't any baby-sitters available at first, but a sub volunteered at the last minute, somebody who knew somebody who knew somebody. Megan was excited about all the attention, believe it or not, begging for room service sand-wiches and a movie to watch while we were out, *Indiana Jones and the Temple of Doom,* if possible.

The sitter came to the door, and she seemed nice. Megan bounced over and took her hand and they were making a tent out of the bed before we even got out the door.

We found the restaurant, Chez something, and the amazing thing is that it was good. They had steak and potatoes and rolls and raspberry tarts with cream—what more could you ask? Well, Mom and Dad and Julie asked for different stuff, but that was their problem. Then I went to the bathroom and it was kind of dark and dirty, and I heard a car backfiring out in the alley and I thought about the explosion. Then I started remembering all the stuff we had seen in the Tower and the museums, the weapons and the instruments of torture. They hurt a lot of people back in the old days, not just on the battlefield, either. Beheading seemed like the easiest way to go, even if you didn't deserve it. Now you had the option of getting blown up at random—or on purpose, if you stupidly got involved.

By this time I was back at the table not listening to Mom and Dad and Julie plan the future, but thinking about the baby-sitter. And I got this creepy feeling, like who was she and why did she volunteer at the last minute? Anybody could say they were a baby-sitter and walk off with my little sister. She'd follow them in a minute if it meant having an adventure like her beloved hobbits. And anybody who had hold of my little sister wouldn't have to worry about my identifying anybody at any time ever. Mom told me to stop squirming, but I couldn't. I practically dragged them out of the restaurant, and they were laughing, trying to keep up with me back to the hotel. When we unlocked the hotel room door, everything was dark except for the TV flickering. The sitter was there, waiting with her coat on to go home, and Megan was a little heap asleep in the bed. I kind of slumped onto my cot, feeling like a fool, but also feeling like the world would never be safe again.

We settled Julie into her apartment the next day and said good-bye. I could tell she was excited to be on her own, except for some messy roommates, but when we left, Megan started to cry and Mom got teary-eyed and Dad blew his nose and when I looked back, Julie was kind of waving out the window like she wasn't sure about the whole thing. It was hard to tell, though, through the rain. While we were packing up that night for the plane ride to Ireland, we got a call from Dan the detective. Had anyone tried to contact us, he asked? He also volunteered that there was no new information on the bombing. The bombing. I guess I knew it was a bomb, the TV had said it was, and there had been a piece in the newspaper. I guess I knew it wasn't spontaneous combustion. Somebody had planted a bomb and blown this woman's leg off, a woman just passing by the shops, walking her little dog. She wouldn't be walking along like that anymore, without a leg and without a little dog.

About the only thing Ireland had in common with London was the rain. It was green green green except for the rocks and the ocean, which changed colors from green to gray to blue and back again. It was also not crowded except for cows and sheep getting herded along the road. We had plenty of time to look around because Dad crept the car along, getting used to driving on a different side of the road, something the bus drivers had handled back in London. Plus, there were all these road signs. Megan's favorite was the picture of a car falling off a pier into the water, and mine was a sign that said LOOSE CHIP- PINGS. For some reason, that struck me as funny. I guess it meant be careful of sliding around on the gravel where they fixed the narrow roads, but it seemed like more than that, like the world had come loose and chips of it were flying around and it might be a good idea to duck the debris, or maybe we were all losing it, like you've lost your chippings, man.

Mostly we ate pub food, which was great, nice simple cheese sandwiches, no more fancy restaurants. We did end up in jail, sort of, when we got to Dublin. Kilmainham Jail, that's where Irish political prisoners had been tortured and shot in the old days. There was a movie about it in the museum and Mom had to take Megan out, because even though this little kid could read about orcs and death riders till the cows came home, she didn't handle real killing very well. The little tin soldiers we played with never screamed or bled. This museum was full of instruments of torture, too. It seemed like a world specialty by this time. Dad talked a lot about Irish history and then we got set to fly again, with Mom slipping her tranquilizers into her purse to get ready for the ordeal.

I figured the Atlantic Ocean was big enough to leave behind what had happened. Dan had our number in the U.S. and I was still a witness, but surely nobody would come looking for me so far away. Three thousand miles passed underneath the plane and I got used to going home, or thought I did. When we loaded our stuff into the cab at O'Hare Airport and started through the

Chicago expressway traffic, it seemed strange, different from when we left. And nobody would believe this, but I missed Julie. I had started thinking about her on the plane and how who- ever had identified me identifying them when their bomb went off could easily have followed us around, and now they knew where Julie lived. She could hear a knock on the door and open it, not knowing who they were.

It seemed like they could find any of us.

Anywhere.

Anytime.

ANGEL

I am what is called a bad girl. You probably know one. We swear, wear indecent clothing, defy authority, and lure innocent boys to their destruction. We appear dumb but most of us are smart enough to beat the system. Not every time. Right now I am in bedroom jail. The innocent boy in question climbed into his window at four A.M. last week after spending some time with me in the park. And of course being clumsy as a toad, he got caught. His parents came to see my father and told him in righteous tones that it was all my fault. Their beloved boy would never do such a thing on his own. That's true. Why would anybody stay out all night just to be by himself? I mentioned that in our little meeting, but they didn't appreciate my logic. I also pointed out that I was the one who made sure he got to school every day instead of getting stoned and dropping out. They didn't appreciate my sense of responsibility, either. We are now forbidden to see each other again. And they wonder why *I'm* so hard to get along with?

"I don't know where you come from," says my father. "Your mother was an angel—"

"*Is* an angel." My mom grew up singing hosanna with the white Presbyterians. Then she married Dad and sang hallelujah with the black Baptists. She's probably a superstar in the heavenly choir.

". . . and I worked too hard to mess around," he adds.

"It just comes naturally, Dad. I'm gifted. They should put me in the fast track."

"You are gifted," he says. "You're a lucky young woman and you are wasting your talents."

"Only some of them," I say. This little scene is played out in our family room, if you want to call it that. I'm sitting there, the dutiful daughter, doing my homework with the TV on and my headphones blasting out some tunes, which I am drowning out with my own vocals, when he comes up behind me and puts his hand on my shoulder. I practically jump out of my skin screaming. "My God, why don't you warn me next time? You scared the sh—"

"Don't say it!" he thunders.

"Okay, you know what you scared out of me."

"Take off those headphones. If you didn't deafen yourself with obscene music, you'd have heard me come home, as I always do at six o'clock."

That's true, my father is a post-office employee and very regular in his habits.

"I sort of lost track of time," I mutter.

"Have you finished your homework?"

"Sure." I cover up the blank sheet of paper.

"I have something to discuss with you."

Oh, great. How I love these little chats about self-improvement—mine, not his. I select my sullen face.

"I've met someone," he says. Just like that. "I've met someone." He sits down across from me on the couch.

"Her name is Sylvia."

Sylvia.

"She's a deacon in the church, and I want you to come with me next Sunday and meet her."

Oh, sure, Dad, just what I'd planned on.

But I go.

She's beautiful, dark like my dad, dignified, old-fashioned, very proper. I mean, gloves and hat. She smiles at me and holds out her hand. What am I supposed to do, spit on it? I shake her hand, limply, and pull on my stone face, firmly. No words necessary. Let her figure out what to say.

"Hello, Marian, I've heard a lot about you."

"I bet." It slips out before I can stop it. Her smile soldiers on.

"Your dad told me you have a beautiful singing voice . . . "

I stare at her. The smile fades a little. The silent stare is a powerful weapon.

". . . just like your mother."

Now she's in for it.

"My mother is dead."

"I know, Marian, your father has told me all about her, as well."

As well? She talks like that, like a school-teacher, but she just works in some candy store.

"I was hoping you'd consider singing in our choir."

Words fail me, and not because I'm trying.

"Well, think it over. Your father has invited me to dinner tonight, so we can talk about it then."

Tonight? He's moving fast. Well, two can play that game, if I ever get away from this sermon. Dad presses down on my knees, which bounce around like kangaroos on speed. Finally, after saying hello to every single soul in the First Baptist Church, we get out of there and I plan my escape based on Dad's ritual Sunday after-noon nap. But instead of changing out of his church clothes, he puts on an apron and starts fixing a pot roast. No no, my kangaroo knees twitch, not an apron, not a pot roast. Yes yes, my kangaroo knees joggle, and he is going to call for help any minute now. Before he can, I volunteer to help if he'll let me out for a couple of hours. Just to the library.

"What will you do at the library?"

"Work on my paper, naturally."

"Alone?"

"Yeah."

"All right, but just there and back again in time for dinner with Sylvia."

He doesn't say what route I have to take there and back again, so I don't even have to lie about going through the park. The park is a place, see, but it's also kind of shorthand for meeting people, especially people my dad wouldn't approve of. And it's Sunday, so there will be a lot of them, all loaded with chemicals to entertain themselves—soft stuff in the daytime, hard stuff at night.

I go the short way to the library, spend twenty minutes checking my e-mail, and head for the park, where my boyfriend just happens to be hanging out, with some weed, because I e-mailed him to meet me there.

We kiss and smoke and kiss and smoke and kiss and smoke some more. Sounds like a song, huh? It's fun, but I have to go. When I stand up, I'm feeling kind of weird.

"Hey, what's in that stuff?"

"It's good, isn't it?"

"It's good for sitting in the park, but I have to go home and be nice at dinner."

I'm swaying by now, and he's not too steady, either, but he helps me get as close to home as he can without risking a sighting by my dad. I manage to get into the door and sneak through the hall toward the stairs. The smell of pot roast is churning around me and I'm taking my first step up, holding onto the banister, when Dad catches me.

"Marian, you're late," he calls. "Come to the table please, we're just starting."

My movement toward the dining room seems to gather a little too much momentum. I try to pause in the doorway and get myself together but somehow I just list forward and start to crumple. My father, who has stood up and moved toward me to pull my chair out, as he does every single night at dinner, gets to me just in time and slides his arm around me so I don't fall too hard.

There is a shocked silence and I don't remember too much of the next bit. Dad says my eyes roll back and he has just decided to call 911 when I come to, throw up, and start raving.

Needless to say, Sylvia goes home.

* * *

"She has some rethinking to do," says my father.

"About what?"

"About our relationship."

"What relationship?"

"Sylvia and I have been seeing each other for some time."

"When?"

"During our lunch breaks, sometimes, and at church. If you came with me regularly, you would have noticed. We enjoy each other's company, although it's perhaps not as challenging as yours."

This quiet little truce comes after the fireworks, when he grounds me forever and arranges for me to stay in an afterschool study program with a female tutor until he gets off work and picks me up.

"So you enjoy each other's company. What's the problem?"

"I'm not sure she's up to the challenge of family living."

"FAMILY LIVING!"

"We were considering marriage."

"And you didn't tell me?"

"We thought we'd wait and see how you two

got along before taking it any further."

"Well, thanks a lot."

"Sylvia and I are fond of each other, Marian, but raising you has always been my first commitment."

Here is where I'm supposed to feel grateful, but it's not happening. Maybe if Dad had another commitment he wouldn't be tracking me down like a bloodhound all the time, like one of those movies where a convict escapes and they set the dogs on him. That's me, teenage convict, with Dad baying on my trail, nose to the ground, ears dangling.

"Marian?"

"What?"

"It might help if you apologized to Sylvia."

Then he walks out of my room. Just like that. And I'm supposed to stay cooped up in here feeling guilty for my sins. Well, you know where he can stick that idea.

Things get worse. My grades come. My boyfriend gets tired of waiting around for me. It's nothing personal, he says, but you're always grounded. Never mind that half the time it's because of him. But well, I'm just no fun.

Plus, my dad really gets sad. He's never been exactly a barrel of laughs, but now he looks kind of beat-up, soul-wise, like the bloodhound got hit by a car. Or like when Mom died. No fits, no fury, just sad, sad, sad. This goes on till I cave.

"So what's happening with Sylvia?" I ask him one night.

He clears his throat and puts down the newspaper, which he hides behind like it was a camouflage outfit.

"She has decided we need a cooling-off period."

"What the f—"

"Don't say it," he says automatically.

"Sorry, what does she mean?"

"Sylvia was deeply disturbed that you would think so little of me—and her—as to appear in the condition you did. It does not, she feels, bode well for our future, and I would have to agree with her."

I'm trapped. I am going to have him on my hands forever. We'll probably go to the senior prom together.

"Okay, I'll apologize."

He looks at me, almost hopeful but not quite. He's scared to be hopeful. I'm a little scared, too, because I did that to him. It's power over my life I want, not power over his.

We call on Sylvia. Those are his words, call on. It means drop in for a visit that everyone expects. Her apartment is spotless. Whenever she's not working in the candy store, she must be cleaning. I work hard not to say this. Power over my life evidently involves power over what comes out of my mouth, as well as what goes into it. Did I really just think "as well"? Oh, my God, it's contagious.

Sylvia welcomes us like a gracious hostess but looks at me hard. She serves tea, real tea in a teapot, with sugar, milk, and cookies. Homemade. Then she waits. I know this game and I know how to outwait her, but that's not why I'm here. Get it over with.

"I'm sorry I was rude during your visit."

"Rude?"

"Well, out of it. I had something that . . ." How do I say this without getting arrested?

"Yes?"

". . . something that didn't agree with me."

"I think what you did goes beyond rudeness, Marian. I think it endangered you."

Fancy words, but she's tougher than I thought. Under the lavender polyester dress lies smooth and flawless skin of steel.

"I said I was sorry."

"That's all you can do about the past. What about the future?"

My kangaroo knees are beginning to activate. My right one and my left one are fighting to see which one can jiggle faster. I've got to get out of here. And then I have this idea. It just comes to me like a Number One hit on the radio. Something impossible. Something that will never work, but they'll think I tried. It's the only way.

"I'll join the choir."

My father leans back in shock. Sylvia finally smiles.

"That will involve practice," she says, "not just performance."

What have I gotten myself into?

"If you really mean it, you can start tonight."

She means it.

* * *

There's still hope. The music director says I have to try out. I belt out my latest Top Ten favorite. This should jinx the plan.

He doesn't even blink. Solo quality, he says, but you have a lot of work to do. He hands me some sheets of paper.

"I don't read music."

"We'll do something familiar first. Sylvia can help you with them. They're old spirituals."

Spirituals—just what I need, I don't say.

"Listen to a Marian Anderson CD. You're named after her, right?"

She was my parents' hero, not mine, I don't say.

He places me in the choir. Right on the front row, probably so he can keep an eye on me. Sylvia must have filled him in. "Just follow along with us today," he says, and starts everyone warming up. In the middle of all this squawking and warbling I hear a sound, the sweetest sound I've ever heard, come pouring out from behind me, like a hot-fudge sundae melting in my mind. The sound is coming from a weird kid behind me. He looks like a teenage genie with a gold earring in one ear. I can't believe the sound is coming from him. He's got his eyes closed, but when he opens them, he stares right at me and winks. Suddenly I have another reason to join the choir.

The music director must be playing therapist, because the first solo he assigns me starts out, "Sometimes I feel like a motherless child." I look at Sylvia suspiciously, but she's chatting with the woman next to her. Maybe it was an accident. They're working on a whole program of spirituals. In the next couple of weeks we try them out in church and then perform them at other places. I actually practice, right along with Marian Anderson on the CD. She's better than me, but this choir turns out to be hot stuff. I mean, we get *booked*.

The morning of my first solo, the church is packed. My father comes with me early, so he's got a prime-time seat in a pew directly facing me. He's nervous, I can tell. He has been ever since this whole choir thing started. It seems like he's more nervous about me being good than being bad. I guess he's scared it's not going to work.

Me, too. You'd think with all the times I've faced down teachers, coaches, and principals, a bunch of churchgoers wouldn't faze me, but my kangaroo knees are acting up—not jiggles but shakes, like volcanic action, nine on the Richter scale. The part of church that usually takes forever flashes by. The director is motioning me to step forward. Just one step. I've practiced this step. But where's the song? It's gone. I can't find it. It's gone completely from my mind. Marian Anderson, where are you when I need you most? Mom, where the hell are *you*?

And finally she's there, soft around me. My mother. Breathe, she whispers, just breathe. Then the music starts and I hear the song coming out of my mouth. But my mouth is just the pathway. It's coming from somewhere else, some other self, some deep-voiced angel.

Sometimes I feel like a motherless child,
Sometimes I feel like a motherless child,
Sometimes I feel like a motherless child,
A long way from home, a long way from
   home.

Oh bring me back.
A long way from home,
A long way from home.

Sometimes I feel like I'm almost gone,
Sometimes I feel like I'm almost gone,
Sometimes I feel like I'm almost gone,
A long way from home, a long way from
    home.

The choir kicks in behind me, Teenage Genie leading the way, and they lift me up, bring me full circle to the last verse.

Sometimes I feel like a motherless child
A long way from home, a long way from
    home.

I close my mouth on time, for once, and come back to the people sitting in front of me. My father has tears streaming down his face. It's like the sound of me has broken his heart. I've never seen him cry before, even when Mom died. There's this space, then, between the sound and the silence. Then my mouth opens all by itself, I don't mean it to, and I say to him right out loud in front of the whole congregation,

"But I never felt like a fatherless child."

He bows his head, and Sylvia says loud and clear behind me, "Amen." The minister picks it up, "Amen," and the congregation, "Amen, amen," holding up their arms. Then I step back and we go on with the next song, "Amazing Grace," like nothing has happened. But it has, and it is, amazing grace.

UNNATURAL
GUESTS

After my little sister Annabelle died, I began to volunteer as a storyteller for kids in the library. It was my mom's idea. Ma Therapist, I call her, which she doesn't like, but that's what she is and does, twenty-four hours a day. My aunt is a minister and I call her Aunt Divine, which she doesn't mind a bit. Aunt Divine is a real character, just the opposite of Ma Therapist, who's pretty boring, like me. In addition to tending homeless people in a downtown mission, Aunt Divine also takes care of every homeless animal she comes across. And nobody ever gives her any trouble. There's just something about Aunt Divine that makes you behave.

Anyhow, like I was saying, after Annabelle

died, each member of the family was supposed to do something to fill the void in our lives. Ma Therapist figured that volunteering in the library would keep me too busy for the kind of trouble my brother Jimmy Joe specialized in before he turned thirteen, the week of my sister's funeral. Who arranges these things, anyway?

Annabelle was five, the surprise baby trailing me by ten years. She was like Jimmy Joe, always getting into mischief and picking fights and trying to get attention. Wouldn't you know I'd have two bratty younger sibs? Annabelle was maybe even worse than Jimmy Joe. She drove everybody crazy, even Ma Therapist, and sometimes I could hardly stand to be around her. Miss Trouble, I called her, and she hated that. "It's not me," she'd shout, "I'm *good*, I'm *Sweet Annabelle*! It's Mr. Trouble's fault!"

She wouldn't tell us who Mr. Trouble was. Then after she got sick, she was too tired to make trouble and all I wanted was for her to get bratty again, at least tease the dog and cats. The one thing that made her feel better was stories. I guess five is a perfect age for listening to stories. And losing battles with leukemia. Unlike

Annabelle's favorite fairy tales, the good guys don't always win. She just got sicker and sicker. She wouldn't eat anything. My mother even gave her chocolate ice cream for breakfast, but Annabelle didn't eat it. She just let it melt, stuck her finger in it, and drew on the wall. Instead of scolding her, Ma Therapist cried. My father brought Annabelle presents from his business trips, which he took more and more the sicker she got ("He's trying to buy her good health," said Ma Therapist). Aunt Divine lobbied the Lord for Annabelle's recovery. Jimmy Joe set up a dartboard in her room, but then he had to throw the darts for her so for the first time they didn't fight over who won the bull's-eye game. And I told her stories. In the end, the stories were all Annabelle wanted.

The problem was, I didn't know that many. I could remember stuff like the Three Little Pigs, but you can overdose on those easy ones pretty fast. And I couldn't just read to her. She'd glaze over. Sick kids don't have the attention span of healthy ones—regression, Ma Therapist calls it. So I couldn't be looking at a book. I had to watch her face and change the story, pick up the pace when she got bored and slow it down when she got confused and pause when she had pain and make her laugh when she looked sad but let her cry when she needed to. Sometimes cheering up involves a lot of tears. Also a lot of stories. I had to learn a lot of stories. Dewey Decimal number 398.2 on the library shelves. Folktales, fairy tales, myths, and legends. Some she wanted to hear over and over, but toward the end I learned a new one every day. Maybe I hoped it would keep her alive, like Scheherazade satisfying the sultan so he wouldn't chop off her head.

One night this weird thing happened. It was an Arabian kind of night, come to think of it, except I seemed to be rubbing a lamp with no magic in it. This was the last night Annabelle was really conscious. She had asked me to stay with her, so I gave the hospice nurse a break and told her to go nap on the couch for a while. The rest of the family was asleep, or as asleep as any of us got in those days. Annabelle was hooked up to all kinds of tubes. She was drifting in and out, but it was unpredictable. Every time I thought she'd gone to sleep, I'd try to stop and suddenly she'd whimper, hey keep going. It was like a marathon. Did I tell you that I run? I guess the two things I can do in the world are run and tell stories. Ma Therapist says they're both about surviving. Anyway, I hit the wall—about midnight I ran out of energy and stories. You know how hard it is to breathe after too many miles, your body just begs for air. I was begging for stories for my sister when I sensed this presence. Some shapeless thing atomized in the room. It didn't feel like any genie, either; it felt like a black hole. Did I tell you I like astronomy? Okay, I can do three things—stories, running, and stars. The stars have seen everything. They make all our little disasters seem like air. There are a lot of stories about stars, too. Some are myths and some are science, but they're all pretty fantastical.

This shapeless thing in the room was definitely a grown-up story, way too scary for Annabelle. I said, "What are you, what are you doing here?"

Annabelle said, "What?"

"Nothing," I said to Annabelle, "I'm just talking to myself."

"Well, talk to me," she whined. I had just told

her a bunch of long stories in a row, about a highway robber and a changeling and a peddler and a selkie.

"I'm trying," I said to her. "I'd do anything for a story." Then I felt this dark thing slide over, wrap around me like a shawl and disintegrate into my pores, my ears, my mouth, and my eyes. It filled me up. "Come on," said Annabelle, "just make one up."

"Okay," I said, and this story poured out of me. I don't know where it came from, but here it is.

Sweet Annabelle was supposed to clean up her room. First she made the bed and lined up all her stuffed animals in a row. Then she put the books back on the shelf and the toys in a basket. After that, she dropped the dirty clothes in a hamper and straightened her shoes neatly along the wall.

Sweet Annabelle.

Last of all, she turned to tidy up the closet, where she sometimes threw things and closed the door so no one could see them. She was poking around in a pile of old junk when she met

Mr. Trouble. One minute he wasn't there, and the next minute he was.

"Howdy," said Mr. Trouble.

"How'd you do that?" asked Annabelle.

"Do what?" asked Mr. Trouble.

"Show up out of nowhere."

"Oh, that's just a little trick," said Mr. Trouble. "Nowhere's where I come from, so I always show up out of nowhere. I can do lots of other tricks, too." He had a big laugh for such a tiny little person.

"Will you show me some of your other tricks?" asked Annabelle.

"Sure," said Mr. Trouble.

And he did. Mr. Trouble bounced on Annabelle's bed till the pillows rained feathers. He pulled the dog's plumey tail, threw grapes at Annabelle's nice big sister, broke her mother's favorite teacup, and slipped a few quarters off her father's dresser for a treat. After a while Annabelle tried out a couple of Mr. Trouble's tricks. They worked pretty well. So well that Annabelle's mother got worried.

"Annabelle used to be such a *sweet* child," she said. "I just don't know what's gotten into her."

"Whatever it is, we'd better get it out," said Annabelle's father.

"She won't do a thing I tell her to," said her mother.

"She does a lot of things I tell her not to," said her father.

"Maybe," said her older sister, "she needs to go see Aunt Divine."

Aunt Divine lived two bus rides away at the top of an old apartment building with thirteen cats that she had rescued from different alleys and a dog she'd found in the garbage can.

While Annabelle's parents talked to Aunt Divine, Annabelle played one of Mr. Trouble's tricks on the dog.

"Hmm," said Aunt Divine. "I might have to keep this girl the whole weekend."

"Whatever's best for Annabelle," said her mother and father, "is what we should do." As they walked out the door, they called, "Be sweet, now, Annabelle."

Annabelle set in on the cats.

"We need to take a little ramble," said Aunt Divine after a while. "I like to keep my eye on the neighborhood."

"I bet you do," sassed Annabelle.

Annabelle and Aunt Divine set out. The first person they met was young Jimmy Joe throwing rocks off the stoop. One of the rocks fell right at Annabelle's feet.

"Here comes trouble," muttered Aunt Divine. Annabelle looked up. Sure enough, there was Mr. Trouble, peering around the corner and waving at Jimmy Joe with a sly gleam in his eye. Mr. Trouble seemed to know Jimmy Joe quite well.

Jimmy Joe didn't look at Annabelle and didn't say hello to Aunt Divine. He just kept throwing rocks. Every rock got a little closer as they walked away. Annabelle looked back and saw Mr. Trouble reach out and hand Jimmy Joe another rock. Annabelle could hear Mr. Trouble's big laugh as the rock landed behind her. Then she felt a sharp crack on the back of her head.

"Ow!" shouted Annabelle, and she charged back at Jimmy Joe with her fists flying. Jimmy Joe waited for her with his own fists raised and a sly smile on his face.

"Hold it!" roared Aunt Divine. She sounded

like a lion. Annabelle stopped in her tracks, and Jimmy Joe lowered his fists. Mr. Trouble was nowhere to be seen.

"I've got a little present for you, Jimmy Joe," said Aunt Divine.

Jimmy Joe smirked. Aunt Divine pulled a big piece of chalk from the pocket of her old blue dress. Then she turned into the alley. Annabelle and Jimmy Joe followed her and watched while she drew three circles on the sooty brick wall, each circle inside the other, with a dot in the middle.

"There, now you got a real target," said Aunt Divine.

"I got lots of real targets," said Jimmy Joe. "That's just a dumb old wall."

"I bet you can't hit the bull's-eye," said Aunt Divine.

Jimmy Joe fingered one of his rocks, took aim, and fired. He hit the third circle. Annabelle picked up a rock, took aim, and hit the second circle. Aunt Divine found a rock, took aim, and hit the dot in the middle.

"Bull's-eye!" said Aunt Divine, rubbing her hands on her old blue dress. "We'll see how you do tomorrow." She pulled Annabelle around the corner and left Jimmy Joe staring at the target with a rock in his hand.

"You got some practicing to do," she said to Annabelle.

Annabelle scrunched up her fists and moped along behind Aunt Divine. She could see her get farther and farther ahead. She could see Aunt Divine's pocketbook hanging open just a little bit. She could see one coin and then another and several others fall to the sidewalk. Quiet as a cat, Mr. Trouble slipped up beside her, picked up a coin, and winked at her. Annabelle picked up the rest of the coins and put them in her pocket. She caught a flying dollar bill and stuffed that in her pocket, too. A few more dollar bills fluttered toward her like little green birds. She caught them and caged them in her pocket. Mr. Trouble disappeared while Annabelle was leaning over the trail of coins.

When Aunt Divine got to the end of the block where the old man always sat begging, she reached in her purse to give him money. Her hand came out empty.

She turned and waited for Annabelle to catch up.

"Trouble never comes in ones," said Aunt Divine. "My money's gone. I have nothing to give this poor man for his cup of coffee." She looked at Annabelle.

"I guess we better go on home then," said Annabelle.

Aunt Divine sighed. "And to think of those rich, velvety chocolate ice-cream cones in the Sweet Shop, on such a hot day."

Annabelle looked down the shimmery street at the Sweet Shop. She breathed the heat, and it stirred a deep hunger in her stomach.

"Well, I have some money," said Annabelle.

"Oh, we couldn't have ice cream while this poor man goes without his coffee," said Aunt Divine.

Annabelle dropped a quarter in the hat.

"Or the rest of his meal," added Aunt Divine.

Annabelle pulled out a dollar bill from her pocket.

"Even scrambled eggs and toast cost more than that," said Aunt Divine.

Annabelle pulled the rest of the dollar bills out of her pocket and dropped them in the hat.

"Now let's see about that ice cream," said

Aunt Divine. "I expect you still have enough change for two cones."

Annabelle did, exactly. The ice cream melted on her tongue and down her fingers. Chocolate made Annabelle feel frisky. She danced ahead of Aunt Divine all the way home. Then she pranced up three flights of stairs to Aunt Divine's door. And there stood Mr. Trouble. He had a chocolate ice-cream cone in one hand, and he was dipping the fingers of his other hand into it and writing sticky brown words all over Aunt Divine's clean white door.

"You'd better get out of here," said Annabelle. "Aunt Divine's going to be mad when she sees that mess."

Mr. Trouble slurped down the cone and licked his fingers. "She won't know who did it," he said. "She'll think it was you."

Annabelle looked down at her sticky fingers. She could hear Aunt Divine coming up the stairs. Annabelle turned her back on Mr. Trouble and ran down to meet her. Aunt Divine looked up at Annabelle's sticky face.

"What's the trouble, child?"

"Aunt Divine, somebody wrote bad words all over your door."

"Who could it be?"

"I've seen him before. He does a lot of bad stuff."

"It takes one to know one," said Aunt Divine. She huffed and puffed up the stairs until they reached the top landing. Annabelle looked around in all the shadows. Mr. Trouble was gone, but the words were still there.

Aunt Divine looked at them. She looked at Annabelle. Annabelle remembered how Aunt Divine hit the bull's-eye without even trying.

"Don't get mad, Aunt Divine, it's not paint— he just wrote those words in chocolate."

"You better wash them off, then, Annabelle, right now. Before you start target practice. Jimmy Joe's a good shot, and tomorrow's coming up real soon."

Aunt Divine unlocked the door, and Annabelle went inside. She brought out a rag and a pan of water. It only took a minute to wash off the words, but in that minute, there was Mr. Trouble right beside her.

"Howdy," said Mr. Trouble.

"Don't you howdy me," said Annabelle. "You're nothing but trouble."

"It takes one to know one," said Mr. Trouble, and his mouth opened into a big, mean grin. Annabelle squeezed the rag in a tight little ball and threw it right between his teeth.

"Bull's-eye!" yelled Annabelle.

"Did you call me, dear?" asked Aunt Divine from the inside hallway.

"No, ma'am, I was just talking to myself," said Annabelle, looking straight at Mr. Trouble.

But Mr. Trouble was gone. One minute he was there and the next minute he wasn't. Annabelle went inside and closed the door. She had to help Aunt Divine take care of all those animals.

When I finished the story, Annabelle was smiling. "Now I know what to do when I'm in trouble," she said, and she threw the only thing she could reach—a balled-up piece of Kleenex—right at me. I wished so hard, then, that someday she'd get into ordinary everyday trouble again, like writing bad words on the wall. The Kleenex fluttered down before it hit me, and her little white hand fell on the sheets and she went to sleep.

All that seems like a long time ago, and I've been telling stories ever since, especially now in the summer when I'm not in school. Stories kind of get under your skin, and then you can't get rid of them. I don't know whether I was dreaming the night Annabelle died, or calling up a genie. Anyway, the kids at the library like my stories, and I never run out of them. In fact, those stories won't go home. I've got a whole bunch of permanent guests. Unnatural guests, you might call them. They eat with me, sleep with me, run with me, stargaze with me, talk to me, everything but listen to me. I know exactly how the princess felt about that frog. Ma Therapist is proud of me. She doesn't know how crowded my room is. But it's okay, because sometimes Annabelle comes back, too, and even Mr. Trouble, peering around the corner behind her. They all seem to be having a real good time.

SECRET TREES

*I*s *he dead?*

   He seems dead.

   Yes.

The whispering sound came down like rain.

Ches rose from somewhere down under, through layers of darkness toward the surface. He was not swimming. The place where he lay felt too hard for water, but it was wet. Ches groped with one hand. The other did not work. He felt pain and leaves—he was lying on wet leaves.

Remember the dead, remember the dead, murmured the trees.

He was not dead. Why didn't someone help him? With effort Ches opened his eyes. What he saw was red. He lifted the good hand to his head and wiped his eyes. Now he could see, but his fingers were red. He was surrounded by a blur of green and brown. Far away the sky was gray. Then the colors spun like a whirlpool and everything turned black.

Ches woke up to white light, white walls, white sheets, and his father's face leaning over him. His left arm lay stiff in a white cast. A white machine, where he was hooked up by a tangle of lines and tubes, blinked a red eye at him and beeped.

"Chester? Ches, it's Dad."

Ches drifted back and forth between the loud white place and the deep dark place.

"Ches, stay with me. Do you remember what happened?"

"No . . . Mom was driving . . . ," Ches lifted his head. The room whirled white.

"Lie down. You have a concussion and a broken arm."

Ches's father gripped the railing on the steel bed. A ridge of bones stretched the skin across his knuckles. Ches lifted his good hand and looked at it. He counted the fingers.

"What about the others?" asked Ches softly.

"What others?"

"I heard people talking."

"No one else was involved, just you and your mother. You were thrown out of the car. She's . . ." His father's voice fell and he turned his head away. That was fine. Ches did not want to hear about his mother. He closed his eyes. He must have imagined the voices in the woods.

Ches sat down on the ground and leaned against a tree, an oak maybe, twice as big and much older than the others. His left arm itched in the cast. Names and drawings covered the plaster. Kids who never spoke to him wanted to sign his cast, but it didn't last past the first week. He pulled a field guide out of his pocket and turned the pages till he came to a leaf like the ones on the row of trees in front of him. Red maple— *Acer rubrum*. Ches admired the plant classification system. It was neat, like a set of boxes nested inside one another, large to small: division, class, order, family, genus, species, variety. He picked up a foot-long piece of broken branch.

It had offshoots like arms and a knot in the wood that looked like one eye—like that giant who ate Ulysses's men on their way home from the Trojan War. The Cyclops. Ches flinched to think how far behind he was in readings for English class. The wood stared at him. He reached into his other pocket and pulled out an old Swiss Army knife his father had handed him on his birthday.

"Your grandfather's," said his father. "Now that you're thirteen, take care of it." Ches's grandfather was long gone, and Ches's dad rarely spoke of him.

Holding the knife steady with the hand that extended from his cast, Ches used his good hand to open it and began smoothing the wood around the Cyclops eye. Not bad for a one-armed whittler. As he worked, the leaves of the old oak whispered above him and scores of maple trees joined in. Some nearby pines sighed, and a lone weeping willow swirled its long-haired branches to the ground. Ches's mother had had long hair. Beyond the willow, a patch of prairie grass taller than Ches's father waved in the late summer wind. The old bones of a car-struck deer that had staggered from the road lay scattered at the side of the clearing.

Ches knew that some kids were afraid of these woods. A wall of heavy firs stood guard around it. But inside the woods, each tree was friendly in its own way. He never felt fear here, even in the dark, even after the accident. It was getting dark now and he should go, else his father would worry. His father worried so much more since the accident. Ches cleaned his knife on his jeans and closed it carefully. The Cyclops continued to stare at him with a round brown eye. Instead of getting up to leave, Ches stretched out on a mat of pine needles and closed his eyes.

He's here again, again.

He's here again.

Ches knew now that the voices were only in his head, but he didn't mind. They were company. A covey of doves rose together across the glade, a squirrel dashed over the path. Ches could feel himself alone with the trees. It was the way he liked to be.

He cut up a giant white onion, leaning over so he could hold it in place with the fingers of his cast arm. He chopped with his good hand, and the juice stung his eyes as he scooped the pieces into a heavy skillet. While the onion sizzled in olive oil, he peeled six carrots and four potatoes, washed the stew meat, and browned it with the onion. Then he added flour, a can of tomatoes, some stock, thyme, and salt. Not bad for a one-armed cook. While the stew simmered, he went upstairs to his room. One-armed, Ches made the bed. One-armed, he folded and put away the clean clothes his father had piled on the dresser. He straightened his collections of rocks, feathers, and tools and laid the Cyclops beside a roll of sandpaper to work on later.

Then he sat down at his desk and stacked books in the right order to do his homework, easiest to hardest from top down, biology, art, algebra, history, Latin, and English. He browsed through his biology book and tried to think neatly. School really meant nothing to him, and he meant nothing to school. It was something he had to do, somewhere he had to go. Tomorrow's assignment was to propose a "personal science project." Why personal? The great thing about science was impersonality. Plus, his teacher required them to do a project involving all their other subjects. Science doesn't sit on a shelf, it's part of life—quote, unquote. Ches liked science on a shelf. It was neater that way.

Well, he could do volcanoes. There was always someone demonstrating volcanic action in the Lab School. He drew a volcano on his cast. The smell of stew floated up the stairs into his room. His left arm ached. His head ached. Ches wished he were back in the woods again. Camping out. Eating stew. Beside the volcano he drew a tree. Why were the trees planted so close together like that?

The bell screamed a command for all students to move quickly. The pure loudness of it pushed everyone through the halls. Ches slowed down and concentrated on closing out the sound. He would rather miss the bus than race along like a lemming. Now he could walk the long way home and stop in the woods. He had made the woods his official personal science project. That made it homework, something to disarm his father's arsenal of worry.

As soon as Ches ducked under the branches

that formed a tunnel through the dark firs, he took a deep breath and felt as if he were breathing for the first time that day. He slid his backpack down under the big oak near the maples, unzipped the side pocket, and pulled out a measuring tape. From the middle section of the backpack, he pulled a notebook and pencil. Then he walked over to a fallen tree and began to measure it, holding the end in place with the fingers of his cast arm and pulling the tape around with his other hand: forty inches around the stump, twenty-four around the top that was lying on the ground.

There was a pathway of broken trees here, made by some long-ago tornado. The top part of the tree, which had twisted and snapped off, was thirty-six feet long. From the ground to the splintered end left standing was ten feet, so forty-six feet added together. All the trees standing nearby looked about the same height and circumference. Ches walked slowly along the first row. The trees were four to five feet apart. Hardly any light could get through, and trees need light. They were strangling. He counted the trees in each row along the length and width of the square maple grove, twenty each way, for a total of four hundred trees, minus a few destroyed by the tornado. There were smaller groves of different species. He needed to make a map.

Ches took a leaf and went back to his oak tree. White oak—*Quercus alba*. From here he could sketch the shape of the maple trees and draw the leaf. The trees would look different when their leaves dropped. He would draw them again then. The leaves hadn't started to show fall colors yet, but soon they would. Even now they were beginning to dry out and rustle, though they weren't saying anything in particular today. They were just chuckling a little, maybe at him and his personal science project.

From the front door, Ches could smell leftover stew heating up, and on his way past the dining room, he saw that the table was already set. He put down his backpack at the bottom of the stairs and washed his hands in the bathroom across the hall. Coming into the kitchen, he almost bumped into his father, who was carrying a bowl of salad in one hand and a basket of bread in the other.

"Ches! Where were you? Get some milk for yourself and light the candles. We're going to eat early."

"We don't need candles, Dad, it's still light outside."

His father lit the candles himself and began to serve the bowls of stew as soon as they sat down. "How was your day?" he asked.

"Okay."

"You were late."

"I stopped by the woods."

"Well, leave a note next time."

"I walked right there from school. I'm working on a science project."

"In the woods?"

"About the woods. Who owns it?"

"The university owns all that land. They're probably going to build a golf course out there."

"You mean, where the woods are?"

"I'm just guessing. It's easy to imagine some deal between Leisure Studies and Park Management and a corporation that reels out big grant money."

"So they'd cut down the trees?"

"That's the trend, but I have no idea. English

professors are not privy to campus planning."
His father speared salad with a fork. "All I know
about trees is a sentimental poem by Joyce
Kilmer. We had to memorize it in school—'I
think that I shall never see a poem lovely as a
tree.' Ogden Nash wrote a spoof on it—'I think
that I shall never see a billboard lovely as a tree.
Perhaps, unless the billboards fall, I'll never see a
tree at all.' I learned that one, too, and when I
stood up to recite the poem I got the two ver-
sions mixed up."

Ches knew he was supposed to laugh at
this story, but he only watched the wax drip
over the brass candlestick into strange shapes.
Moonscapes. A candle guttered in the breeze
that swept through the windows.

"How's your arm? You're using it a lot," said
his father.

"It's fine. I'd like to get the cast off."

"Soon, another two weeks."

Ches stood up to clear the table.

"I'm going to see your mother tonight," said
his father. "I'd like you to come with me."

Ches walked over to the stairs, scooped up
his backpack on the way, went up to his room,

and shut the door. After a while he heard his father drive away. He picked up the Cyclops and began to sand it smooth. He felt sorry for the Cyclops, the way Ulysses had blinded its one eye to escape the cave. Of course, if Ulysses had not tricked it, the Cyclops would have eaten him. It was not easy being Ulysses, but it was not easy being a Cyclops, either.

On Saturday morning, Ches ducked through the fir tunnel and started toward a new grove, the thorny honey locust trees he had identified yesterday—*Gleditsia triacanthos*. As he rounded a row of maples, he suddenly stood face-to-face with an old man. Both of them took a startled step backward.

"Whoa, boy, you scared the daylights out of me."

Ches said nothing.

"I don't get too many visitors."

"You own these woods?"

"No, but I come here just about every day."

"Me, too."

"How come I've never seen you?"

"I mostly come after school."

"I come early in the morning. It's a nice walk from where I live, over there in the world's greatest retirement community."

"Yeah, I pass by it walking home from school."

"I'll tell you the truth—the only great thing about it is being near these trees. That batch over there was my dissertation."

"Those honey locusts?"

"How'd you know?"

Ches showed him the field guide. "Did you study honey locusts?"

"Plant pathology. We were working on the state natural history survey. I planted those about fifty years ago. That grove of mountain ash over there was my best friend's project. *Sorbus americana*. It's not a true ash but related to hawthorns and apples. It gets nice red berries for the birds. There's a European species, the rowan tree, that's supposed to protect you against bewitchment." The old man paused. He had a slow way of talking, like he was thinking between words, and he moved slowly as if it hurt him to move.

"Did it?"

"Did it what?"

"Protect your friend against bewitchment?"

The old man smiled. "Maybe. He went to the West Coast and taught for thirty years. Now he's six feet under. Buried beside a tree, I hope."

"These trees were all students' projects?"

"Students' and professors'. We worked together out here. Not to be nosy or anything, but what happened to your arm?"

"I had an accident. Why did you plant the trees so close together?"

"We were trying to stress them. Deprive them of light and nutrients. We inoculated them to see how they'd withstand stress-related diseases."

"You gave them diseases on purpose. . . ." Ches looked startled, but the old man did not notice. He was inspecting the trees.

"Yeah, borers, fungus. We wanted to test how susceptible they were, planted close like that."

"They're still here," said Ches.

"Some are in better shape than others. We were doing this to help us understand suscepti-bility and resistance, like I said—for the sake of future trees."

"What about the old oak? It looks okay."

"That was already here, and the weeping

willow, that big sycamore, the apple trees, all those were here when it was a farm. Before it was a farm, some of them. We put in those rows"—and he named the trees like old friends—"honey locust, ash, hemlock, pine, juniper, cedar, birch, hickory, walnut. I'm forgetting some now."

Ches pulled out the map of trees he had made—diseased trees, he realized now, not neat at all. But he had to do a science project. "Could you help me with this?"

The trees stood quietly. There was no wind, just the two human voices, one high and the other low.

Ches slipped downstairs into the kitchen and took the biggest apple from the bowl on the counter. He bit into the apple on his way through the hall. At the door he stopped and went back for another apple. Then he left the house and walked toward the woods. His father had come home late the night before. Ches had been careful to leave a note saying he was going out early.

The dawn air was cool. Dew was heavy on the high grass, and his shoes and pants were soaked after a few steps. The maple grove was deserted, but in the middle of the honey locust trees, Ches found the old man standing straight and quiet, facing east. He had a solid build, white hair, and bronzed, creased skin, as if he had spent a lot of time out in the wind.

Golden light spiked the clean prairie sky. Ches moved to the old man's side just as the full circle of the sun lifted off the horizon at the edge of the woods.

"A man of your word," said the old man, "right on time. Did we swap names yesterday?"

"It's Ches. Chester Hayes."

"I'm Walter Hill." He stretched out a gnarled hand and Ches shook it. "Hayes and Hill. Sounds like a law firm," said the old man. "I guess we should make that a tree firm."

Chester gave him a rare smile that lit up his shadowy brown eyes for a second before fading under the thatch of brown hair falling over his forehead. He pulled the map out of his pocket as they walked away from the honey locust trees.

"The book had a picture of these—dawn redwoods?" asked Ches.

In front of them, each tree of the single row towered to a triangular point above them. One had been snapped off by the tornado about a quarter of the way up the trunk, which left a hole in the row like a broken tooth.

"Yep, *Metasequoia glyptostroboides*—related to the cypress family, Taxodiaceae. They're deciduous conifers. That means all those feathery green needles are going to fall into a big yellow heap come November, or whenever the cold weather sets in."

Ches leaned over and picked up a small cone.

"That holds its seeds, like the honey locust pod I showed you yesterday," said the old man.

"What were you testing these for?" Ches asked suspiciously.

Walter Hill looked at him for a long time. "You know," he said finally, "that's a good question, but it was our question and I suspect it's not really yours. For this tree, we just wanted to measure its growth rate here in Zone 6. I can tell you all about our research, and you can put it in your report. But I always ask my students—used to ask my students—what's the question you're asking when you start a project. What's your goal?"

"My goal is to pass biology."

"I expect it's more than that."

"Yeah, I have to include all my other subjects—art, math, history, Latin, and English. So I'm drawing and carving and calculating and mapping with scientific names—they're all in Latin. You're telling me about the history."

"What about English?"

The old man was very systematic, thought Ches. "That's writing up the project, I guess. My dad teaches poetry. He could help me find some poems, but . . ." Ches trailed off.

"You don't want any poetry."

"No. I just want to do the trees."

"What would you do with the trees if they were yours?"

"Just leave them like they are."

"It's not a natural forest growth. They'd be healthier if you thinned them, take some out of each row and give them some growing room."

"Why doesn't the university do that?"

"Our experiments are long over, and the new folks don't have time or money to throw away."

"It wouldn't be thrown away!"

"Who else comes here besides you and me?"

"Well, they could make it into a tree museum or something."

"An arboretum."

"Yeah."

"They could, but I suspect it's not a high priority. Besides, you'd lose your retreat. These trees are kind of a secret the way they are now."

"Kind of a sick secret," said Ches. It was sad about the trees, stressing them on purpose and then just letting them die. The more he thought about it, the sadder it seemed. He was starting to wish the old man would shut up and go away instead of droning on about diseased trees and scientific questions.

Finally Walter Hill wound down. "You think about it. I'll help you out if I can, but your work won't mean much unless you figure out what you're looking for."

They walked through the pines, gleaming silent in the sunlight, then turned to go their own ways. Ches thanked the old man before starting home, but the interest had seeped out of his project. What had been mysterious now seemed creepy. It was better when he came here by himself and listened to the trees. Ches shoved his hand into the pocket of his fatigues, found the apple he'd brought for the old man, and tossed it into the glade to seed itself. The firs slapped his face as he left the woods through their tunnel of branches.

His arm felt weightless after the cast was cut off, the skin newly aware of the air and paled to a lighter shade than his hand. At first he kept his arm close to his body, but soon it moved of its own accord. His teacher asked him to hand out some tests to celebrate his freed arm.

The class groaned or gloated over the questions. Ches answered them automatically.

That afternoon he sneaked into the woods as if someone were following—or waiting for him. He sat down on the log. Looking around, Ches wondered how many trees had snapped because they were weakened by disease.

Many others, many others, whispered the leaves all around.

Without warning, his mother walked into his mind, passing through a locked door. Her eyes were leaf green, her hair the brown of bark—a mirror image of Ches. She did not speak. Only the trees spoke.

Many others.

* * *

"Chester?" asked his father. It was a request to enter. Ches looked up as his father opened the bedroom door.

"You could knock," said Ches.

"All right, next time." His father stood there awkwardly.

"Did you need me?"

"I found something you might want to read. About those trees."

"What is it?"

"Your mother was working on some new poems. I hesitated to show this to you. It's obviously an unfinished draft, just first thoughts, and Laurel never showed anyone her work until it was polished. But I think this one's about those woods you're researching."

"I'm not doing that project anymore."

"Why not?"

"It was a stupid idea."

"You seemed excited about it."

"Not anymore."

"Are you doing something else?"

"I'm studying right now."

"I can see that. I meant, have you chosen another project?"

"No. I'll figure out something. Volcanoes, maybe."

His father started to turn away, but instead crossed the room and laid a single sheet of paper on the desk. "You might want to read this anyway." Then he left, closing the door behind him.

Ches crumpled up the paper and dropped it in the wastebasket, but not before he glimpsed the title, "Sylvan Suburbs." After that he got up and locked the door.

Every day Ches came straight home from school and sat at his desk beside the wastebasket that held the crumpled paper. He worked ahead in every subject, as if he had to pass a test that would save his life. Sometimes he sanded the Cyclops, but he stopped for fear he would sand it away. The wood was smooth as honey now, glowering at him with its round brown eye. The body curved to fit his hand, and the arms that reached out were silken instead of ending sharp and broken. He needed to carve something else, but he didn't want to visit the woods too often, not with the old man waiting to talk about sick trees and ask about his goals.

Day after day Ches studied beside the crumpled

paper. Once he almost burned it, striking a
match and holding it over the metal wastebasket. He blew out the match when it burned
down to his fingertips. One night, after finishing
the algebra, history, Latin, and even English
assigned for the next week, he sat sketching his
ideas for art class. The drawing pad filled with
trees, row after row of needled or leafy trees.
Finally, he stretched his hand down, picked up
the crumpled paper, and smoothed it out.

Wasn't there a word, once, to describe woods?
Was it *sylvan*? Weren't the trees, once, never
planted like rows of corn, and didn't grasses
stretch sunward as far as possible? Don't ghosts
of all those growing flora haunt the houses,
reaching farther than possible across a plain
that's paved, now, so water never seeps to
 the roots?

Must we live in a suburb of sylvan ghosts,
our lumbered lives silent in the shadeless light,
so separated from our natural state that
listening finds no whispering in leafless
winds? Must we live

* * *

The poem stopped there. Was it unfinished or asking a question no one heard his mother ask?

As soon as Ches heard his father drive away, he closed his Latin book and stared back at the Cyclops living in its cave on a shelf in the corner of his room. It was almost dark outside. Ches had never visited the woods at night, but it was the perfect time. The old man wouldn't be there, and Ches could get back before his father came home. He looked around for his flashlight—in his room, downstairs in the kitchen. His father had probably borrowed it. His father was always losing things. Then Ches saw the candles on the table—the candles his mother had always lit at dinner, staring at the flame sometimes instead of eating her food. He took one of the red candles out of its brass holder and stuck the box of matches in his pocket. Then he carefully locked the door behind him and set out into the night.

The old gravel road that led to the woods glowed in the moonlight, but when he turned to duck through the hemlocks, darkness slowed him. He felt the pathway more than saw it. As if his feet had eyes, they led him toward the old oak and the maple log nearby. His own cave. Carefully clearing away a circle of dead leaves and twigs, he centered the candle in the earth and struck a match. The candlelight filtered the dark without closing it off the way a flashlight would do.

Once again, Ches's mother appeared, infiltrating his cavelike space and staring at the candlelight as she had done at the dinner table, hypnotized by its constant flickering movement. This time, Ches let her stay. He felt himself staring at the candlelight. He felt peace like a pillow as he curled up on his side with his head resting on his arm.

The candlelight quivered, the night noises rustled, and the trees whispered.

Sleep.

I can't go to sleep, thought Ches. Dad will come home and find me gone. But just a little longer. A light wind like his mother's fingertips lifted his hair. He was surprised to find her still there, with the trees rustling all around them.

Just a little longer.

* * *

Ches jerked awake. What? What? Light flared in front of him and warmed his face. He sat up and saw that the wind had blown some leaves across his tiny cleared circle. The candle had burned to the ground and lit the leaves. He jumped up so suddenly that dizziness flickered around his eyes and head. With both feet he stamped on the fire and when it was out, he stared down at the neatly blackened circle as if it were still burning. An ugly smell of singed sneaker soaked the air. Ches turned and ran through the woods, branches whipping his face. He hurtled through the hemlocks and along the gravel road toward home. Frantically he searched his pocket for the key and found instead a box of matches. Then the other pocket, the key, the door. The house was dark.

Ches raced through the hall and up the stairs, not stopping till he reached his room and locked the door behind him. Through the open window he heard the automatic garage door lifting as his father's car crunched up the short driveway. Ches stripped off his leafy clothes and threw them in back of his closet. He pulled on a clean T-shirt, dove into bed, and pulled up the sheet around his neck. There were footsteps on the old wooden stairs, a soft knock at his door, and then creaking hallway floorboards as his father walked slowly toward his own room. It was a long time before Ches's heart stopped shaking his body, and even longer before he could stamp out the fire in his mind and wait for sleep.

Then came his mother again. Somehow his mother had followed him home. He did not allow his mother to come into his room, but here she was, picking him up from school last spring. He buried his head under the pillow, but she was opening the car door and he was stepping inside.

"Let's get your hiking stuff today," she said. She almost sang it. "Camp's just around the corner. No more classes, no more books . . ." She paused, then her face collapsed like a fallen building. "What's the rest of it?" she asked. "I can't remember. What's the rest of it, Ches?"

"I don't know, Mom."

"It used to rhyme. I used to say it. I can't remember the words. The words are not coming anymore."

Ches wished he had taken the bus. His

mother pulled out of the line of waiting parents and plunged into the traffic. She swerved around the slow cars and began to speed toward the highway. Her hands gripped the wheel as if the world depended on their forward motion.

"Mom, where are we going?"

She didn't answer but began to stare through the windshield, not downward toward the road but upward toward the afternoon sun in the same way she stared at the candlelight during dinner.

"Mom?"

She pressed her foot harder on the accelerator and shot onto the expressway, barely squeezing between an SUV and a van. The SUV honked and pulled into the next lane to pass her, the driver glaring out the side window. Ches's mother followed into the next lane, staring and staring ahead, with only a few feet between her and the SUV.

Ches groped for the seat belt he had forgotten to put on and glanced at his mother. "Mom, slow down! Your seat belt . . . "

Without looking at him, his mother took both hands off the wheel and reached behind her for the seat belt, as if they were still waiting in line back at the school, as if she had not even started the car yet. Freed to follow the tilting surface of the road, the car began to veer across the median. A truck loomed toward them. Ches reached over and grabbed the steering wheel, twisting it back toward their side of the road. The car crisscrossed the highway again, just missing the van, careened toward the roadside, over the shoulder, and plunged into the woods beyond, into the trees planted like rows of dark green corn, into the sylvan suburbs.

Not once had his mother looked at him. Now here she was, finally looking at him, and she wouldn't go away.

The next day after school Ches sat hunched over his desk, propping his tired head up by leaning his forehead on one hand. Rather than staying neatly in line, the numbers and letters on a page of algebra problems jumbled into some unknown language. Downstairs he heard the doorbell ring.

Ches slipped down the stairs, opened the door, and looked into the neat plaid pattern of Walter Hill's flannel shirt.

"Hello, Ches, remember me? I thought I'd drop by and see how your science project is coming along. Haven't seen you in the woods lately."

"I'm . . . I guess I'm changing topics."

"Is that right? Well, somebody's going over there. I was walking by the big oak this morning and found signs of a campfire."

Ches said nothing.

"University students, maybe?" the old man asked. Then he frowned. "You'd think they'd know better, wouldn't you? Lighting a fire in the middle of dry woods like that . . . and people mostly stay away from there." He locked eyes with Ches, who stared back as if hypnotized.

"No beer cans or cigarette butts. Just this." The old man pulled a chunk of melted red candle wax out of his pocket and held it out to Ches.

Ches's arms stayed rigid at his sides, and he dropped his eyes.

"Are your folks home, by any chance?" asked the old man.

"No."

"You said your dad works for the university?"

"Yes."

"Well, I'd like to meet him. I thought we should get a little better acquainted if we're going to take on this science project—if you haven't given up on it, that is."

Ches looked up, finally, and saw that Walter Hill, the most ordinary-looking person in the world, was smiling at him. His eyes wrinkled up at the corners as if he were squinting at the sun. Ches surprised himself and stepped back. "Would you like to come in?" he asked.

"Thanks, I'd appreciate sitting down for a spell. Arthritis has stiffened up these knees. I didn't really expect to come this far when I started out."

As Ches walked him through the hall, he saw the old man glance to the right, into the dining room, where two candlesticks stood on the table. One was empty. The other held a candle that matched the melted red wax in Walter Hill's pocket.

Walter Hill was such an outdoor person that Ches could hardly imagine him being anywhere else. It seemed natural to walk him out to the old screened-in back porch. There was a rocking chair there, alongside a porch swing, and the late-afternoon sun softened the green yard around them. The old man settled into the rocking chair as if he did it every day. Ches swayed in the porch swing. They both looked out on the trees, old sycamores and hemlocks, a few small dogwoods. They rocked and swayed, and the movement eased their silence from stiff to relaxed. Ches felt his mother glide onto the porch and take her place on the swing.

"I used to sit here with my mother," said Ches. He was startled to hear his own voice.

"Did you?" asked Walter Hill.

"When I was little." Ches could feel his mother's arm slip around his shoulders. She must like Walter Hill, to come and sit with them like this.

"Not anymore?"

"No, she's dead."

"I'm sorry to hear that."

They swayed and rocked a while longer.

"My wife and I had a porch swing," said Walter Hill. "We used to swing on it every evening after supper, unless it was cold. In cold weather we built a fire in the fireplace and sat around watching it. A fire kind of hypnotizes you, doesn't it?"

Ches nodded. "My mother . . ."

Walter Hill suddenly looked up. Ches's father stood in the back doorway with a pizza box in his hand and a puzzled expression on his face.

Ches jumped up. "Dad, this is Walter Hill. He used to do research on the trees where I started my science project."

Walter Hill stood up slowly, pushing on the arms of the rocking chair, and held out his hand. "Hello . . ."

"I think we met once. At a reception for your distinguished service award. I'm Douglas Hayes, in the English department. Head of the English department."

"Nice to meet you. I retired from biology. Ches and I met in the woods, but I haven't seen him lately, so I thought I'd check up on how he was doing with his project."

"He seems to have given it up."

"I wasn't sure, Dad, I was just . . ."

Ches's dad waited for the end of the sentence. Then he switched the box of pizza to his other arm. "Well," he said awkwardly, "would you like to join us for dinner, Dr. Hill? We're just going to have a quick bite. I have to leave again a little later." Ches's father led the old man through the kitchen into the dining room while Ches grabbed plates and filled glasses with iced tea. As the three of them sat down, Ches's father picked up the candle and looked around the table. "That's odd. Where's the other candle, Ches, and the matches?"

"I, uh, borrowed them for an experiment, Dad." Ches did not look at Walter Hill.

"Well, you know to be careful," said Ches's father. "I'm sorry I have to go out again tonight, but I'll try to get back early." He pulled apart two fat pieces of pizza, trailing some strings of cheese.

"Could I be of service?" asked Walter Hill.

"Actually, Ches is used to this." He paused. "My wife is undergoing treatment at the Providence Center. She had a mental breakdown, and there was an automobile accident involved. Fortunately she had no physical injuries, and Ches has recovered from his."

Ches chewed on a wad of cheese and crust that would not go away.

"I see," said Walter Hill. "Well, I'd rather keep Ches company than spend the evening with my TV set."

"How about it, Ches?" said his dad.

Ches looked at the empty candleholder and then at his father. "I have a lot of homework to do. There's an algebra test tomorrow."

"I'm pretty good at algebra. Maybe I can help," said Walter Hill. He, too, glanced at the empty candleholder.

Finally Ches raised his eyes to meet Walter Hill's. "Maybe you can."

After Ches's father left, Walter Hill said nothing about anyone's goals or anyone's family. He just settled down at the kitchen table and helped Ches do his homework.

"Seems like you already know this pretty well," he said as they worked through the algebra problems.

"I like algebra."

"Also science, Latin, history, and art, as I recall. Everything except English."

"You remember a lot."

"Biologists have to memorize stuff. You train yourself. But I'm slipping every day. In a couple of years I won't remember to flush the toilet."

Ches smiled. Then he stopped smiling as the bathroom door slammed in his face and his mother locked it. He stood there, listening. It seemed like he stood there for hours. She didn't flush the toilet. She just cried.

"Ches?"

"Yeah, I'm here. I just remembered something."

"You have anything else to do in the homework department?"

"No, I'm done."

"Maybe you better get some sleep. You look kind of tuckered out."

"Okay." Ches gathered up his book and papers.

"I guess you're too old for reading aloud," said Walter Hill.

"I guess!"

Walter Hill smiled. "Don't be insulted. I used to read aloud to my wife every night. But I'll read to myself this time. Looks like there's plenty to choose from." He glanced at the bookshelves lining the hallway they were passing through.

"If you like poetry and critical theory." Ches turned up the stairs.

"I do like poetry, actually," said Walter Hill. "I'll leave the critical theory to your dad. Good night, Ches. Sweet dreams and all that."

"Night," said Ches. He wished for no dreams. He was still awake enough to hear voices when his father came home. The voices rumbled on for quite a long time, but he was too tired to get up and eavesdrop.

During the next few weeks Ches worked in the woods with Walter Hill almost every day. They carried out Ches's plan of mapping the groves. They checked trees for damage by disease, lack of light and nutrients, lightning or wind. Ches tape-recorded an interview with the old man, who described in detail the reasons for what was planted where, and when. Ches pressed leaves, brilliantly colored now, and sketched the shapes of fully developed trees, a model for each species—the swaybacked hemlocks, the fat oaks, the raggedy nut trees.

He and Walter Hill spent most of their time in friendly silence, with only the trees talking. Some tattled and rattled their dry leaves. Others whispered through needle-sharp teeth or gave a throaty roar in the fall winds. Walter Hill did not challenge Ches about what question he was asking with his project, and Ches was content to create an illustrated catalog of the woods.

The Saturday before the project was due, he put it all together, mounting his maps and drawings on posterboard. He revised the narrative on his computer and displayed pressed leaves on trays covered with plastic. He arranged samples of wood, from light and smooth to dark and heavily grained. He added the carved Cyclops, just for fun. Then he invited Walter Hill to come upstairs to his room for a preview. They looked at the work for a long time.

"You've done well, Ches. What does your dad say about this masterpiece?"

"He's not home."

"Ches?"

"What?"

"Did you ever think about going with him?"

Ches's face turned stony. "No."

"Well, think about it."

"He could stay home with me every once in a while."

"He could. I'm just asking you to think about it for your own sake."

Ches turned away and looked at the glowering Cyclops. Walter Hill put his hand on Ches's shoulder and, when Ches shrugged it off, retreated from the room. The preview of Ches's science project was over.

The car crawled along so carefully that Ches felt like screaming. He sat as far from his father as the front seat would let him and looked out the side window. Beyond the housing developments packed near the road, flat fields stretched as far as he could see, one after the other, with few trees to relieve them. *Must we live in a suburb of sylvan ghosts?* Why was he doing this? Because some stupid old man had told him it was a good idea. Because the science project was over and the prize he had won came and went, leaving him with nothing else to do. Because he had to know, finally, where she had gone and why she had left him. *Your work won't mean much unless you figure out what you're looking for.*

The old man still rang the doorbell sometimes, but Ches did not feel like answering. The only one who stayed with him now was the Cyclops, back from its conquest at the science fair, ugly as always.

Suddenly they were there, parking beside a place that looked too old for automobiles. It was a big gray stone building surrounded by bare trees. They had to check in at a desk that guarded two locked doors.

"She's waiting for you, Professor Hayes, as always."

"Thanks, Mrs. Perry. This is my son, Ches."

The plump, comfy-looking receptionist named Mrs. Perry gave Ches a sympathetic smile. "Glad you could come with your dad today."

Without a word, Ches turned to follow his father as the doors buzzed open. He wished Mrs. Perry would drop into the churning, red-hot magma of a volcano. He wished someone would hold his hand.

Ches walked behind his father down a long hall-way with numbered doors on each side. At the end of the corridor, an attendant looked up from her desk, smiled at his father, and turned back to her paperwork. When they came to Room 105, his father waited for Ches to catch up and then knocked on the door. No one answered, but he turned the handle and entered.

"Laurel?" he said. "It's Douglas."

Ches stared into the room. It was lit only by daylight from one window. There was a bed, a small table beside it, a locker, a door into a bare bathroom, an orange plastic chair, and a beige armchair in the corner. Curled up in the armchair was a small figure, not the mother he remembered, but someone who looked like a child. She was thin, pale, her brown hair pulled straight back. Since she was staring out the window, he could not see her eyes.

"Laurel, I brought you a surprise."

Ches's mother did not speak or move or turn to look at Ches or his father. She continued to stare out the window as if hypnotized. When Ches looked where she looked, all he saw was the trunk of one of the tall bare trees that surrounded the parking lot.

Ches's father motioned him over to stand in front of her. He stood first to the side and then directly in front of her, blocking her vision out the window.

"Mom?"

She continued to stare as if he were not there.

Ches's father took her hand. "Laurel, say hello, Ches is here. I know you've been missing him."

His mother stayed curled up and frozen.

Ches's father shook his head. "I'm sorry, Ches, sometimes she's better and sometimes worse. Last time I was here, I read to her and she seemed to enjoy it."

Ches looked down at the stranger who was his mother. Standing in front of her now, he could see her eyes. Her eyes were holes. She was hollow, her heartwood crumbled away. He turned and walked out of the room.

"I'm sorry, Ches. I thought that seeing you would turn her around. I thought she'd respond. She loves you so much." Ches's father leaned his head and arms on the steering wheel in the parking lot. For a moment, Ches thought he was crying, but then he straightened his shoulders and started the car. "Well, we just have to keep trying. They're testing out some new drug therapies."

Ches stared out the window. He wondered if he looked like his mother staring out the window.

* * *

Ches lay, still staring, this time at the ceiling. He felt as if he had been staring forever—out the car window coming back all the way from the hospital, out the school windows every day. He had been lying on his bed ever since his father left on another visit to the hospital. Ches hadn't even done his homework. He had not done his homework for a week, but it didn't matter. He had worked so far ahead that nobody could tell. Ches thought about all the work he'd done on the science project. He glanced over at the Cyclops, staring at him from the shadows with its one eye—everyone was staring. No one was seeing.

Ches remembered how wily Ulysses had tricked the Cyclops by saying his name was No Man. When the Cyclops's friends asked who was hurting him, the Cyclops—now blinded by a burning stake through his eye—replied, "No Man is hurting me." So the friends told him to stop bothering them, and they all went away and left him alone.

Suddenly Ches stood up, strode across the room, and seized the Cyclops. Slipping down the stairs, he grabbed the other red candle still standing in its brass candlestick and the new matches his father had laid beside it. Then he slammed out the door and into the darkening evening. As he ran he felt a swirling inside, a release from all the staring. A chill prairie wind rushed him along. Ches ran faster, breathing hard and pounding down the gravel road that led to the trees. He brushed through the dark tunnel of hemlocks, past the oak, straight into the grove of diseased trees that stretched toward the highway where his mother had veered off the road. The place where she had stopped seeing him forever.

The trees were bare, their branches bony and their rows of trunks standing ankle deep in dead leaves. Even the trees stared at him now. The only sound came from the ground as he stormed through the brittle leaves.

Ches stopped in a drift of brown. First he lit the candle and cradled it with his hand, then he held it to the satiny-soft, seasoned wood of the Cyclops. One arm darkened, flickered, and flared. Holding it like a torch, he touched the leaves all around with the tiny flame till he had a circle smoking around him. Ches backed out of the circle of fire and watched as the wind picked up and blew smoke and flames farther through the woods. He retreated as the fire advanced, pushing him closer and closer toward the highway. The trees hissed and snapped and spat at him. He was watching them burn, with the searing flames reaching for his sneakers and hair when the first fire engine pulled up. Someone grabbed him from behind and pulled him away.

Ches watched as the old man walked slowly toward the desk where a uniformed police officer sat filling out forms.

"I'm Walter Hill," he said slowly. "You called me about a boy named Chester Hayes."

"Over there," said the officer. She gestured toward the corner where Ches sat with another officer. "He told us his father wasn't home, that we should call his grandfather at the retirement home."

"I see," said the old man.

"He says he started the fire on purpose. We'll have to hold him in juvenile detention overnight till we can get one of the social workers over here to evaluate him."

Walter Hill nodded. "I'm sure his father will be home soon. I'd like to stay with him till we can contact him."

"Okay with me," she said.

The old man crossed the room and sat down on the bench beside Ches, who did not look up at him. Ches was staring at the floor. Staring, staring, staring. Then a warm hand folded over his cold one. He shivered, his whole body shaking. He felt an arm around his shoulder, and finally Ches began to cry. He cried and cried into the soft flannel shirt of Walter Hill.

Over and over Ches reread the same sentence beginning his biology assignment. His brain, which used to skim over words, now dragged along and snagged easily, so that he had to go back and start over again. Walter Hill sat across from him, reading. The kitchen table where they worked every afternoon was scattered with books and papers. Ches's parole from juvenile detention was conditioned on his confinement to the house after school with an adult present at all times. Walter Hill had volunteered. When they weren't reading, they argued.

"It's not easy to be head of a department," said the old man. "The university's a corporate world these days. Your father has a lot of meetings. He doesn't sit around reading poetry all day."

"Sure," said Ches bitterly, "and he has my mother to take care of."

"She's mentally ill, Ches. You can't just give up on someone you love."

"He gave up on me."

"He didn't give up on you. He's working hard to be a good father. Maybe he doesn't always know how."

Ches stabbed a notebook with his pen. "And how would you know?"

"I wouldn't. I've never been a father and I'm not trying to be yours. I'm feeling my way here." The old man paused. "My wife and I couldn't have children—we just fed all the students who dropped by."

"So where are they now?" Not visiting you in the retirement home, thought Ches, but he didn't say that. He didn't need to. The old man was lonely but not stupid.

"Oh, they went their different ways. Students

come for a while and go, and that's the way it should be. A few graduate students stay in touch."

Ches stopped rereading the sentence he had been working on before, during, and after their argument. He began drawing in his book, decorating the large capital letter that started the chapter so that it looked like an old manuscript. Vines grew out of the letter, and little faces peered through the vines. Soon the whole margin of the book looked like a miniature jungle.

Walter Hill peered over at his drawing. "Speaking of giving up," said the old man, "just because your science fair project is over doesn't mean you're finished with it."

Ches looked up, shocked, from his textbook graffiti. After admitting that he had started the fire, he had refused to talk about it with anyone, including the therapist he was supposed to see every week. When he thought about the fire, his mind filled with smoke and he stumbled along a pathway where there were no words, only burning anger and shame.

"For instance, you might ask what happens after a disaster," said Walter Hill. "You know,

there's such a thing in nature as a burnover—
prairie fires started by lightning, that kind of
thing. I'm reading a book about Mount St.
Helens, where the environmentalists thought
the volcanic eruption was a catastrophe, but it
turned out to rejuvenate the whole ecosystem.
It's nature's covenant with the future, like a
promise to keep going. Forest rangers do controlled burns sometimes. 'Controlled' is the
operative word there."

Ches smoldered for a while in silence. "Your
trees are dead," he said finally.

"They're our trees," said the old man, "but
we'll see what happens when you get out of
jail—I mean, house arrest. Kitchen confinement." Then he smiled at Ches from his worn-
down face. "Trust me. We'll see," he said again.

Blackened tree trunks leaned or lay across one
another in the slanting gray rain. It was a slow,
cold spring. Yet far below the bleak winds one
stubborn seedling unfolded from its acorn coffin,
buried underground and forgotten by a squirrel.
Several scrawny, pointed needles forked out of
seeds that had exploded from a flaming

pinecone, long cooled. The winged maple pods caught under a rock last autumn pushed sideways around it now with rooted energy. In a tract of land bordered by concrete highways, housing developments, and muddy corn and soybean fields as far as the eye could see grew a wild patch of secret green shoots tipping above the sooty earth like stars flickering awake in an ancient nighttime sky.

PART III
BEYOND PAST AND PRESENT

(SET MOSTLY IN HEAVEN AND HELL)

LIGHT

Everybody expected God to have a Great Dane, maybe, or a German shepherd, a Saint Bernard, a malamute, a mastiff, a Newfoundland, an ancient wolfhound, something noble, powerful, dignified, or even just protective, a Doberman pinscher to keep out the riffraff. Nobody expected a Chihuahua named Beanie. But God had to get into some pretty small places and liked having company. It's not that Heaven was small, God knows, and there was plenty of work to do up there. Some of the souls had a tough transition, leaving behind all that money, or misery, or whatever else they had gotten attached to. And somehow Beanie was a comfort to them. Beanie's little pop eyes and big ears made them smile right from the time they stepped through the pearly gates. He was just such a surprise, almost as much a surprise as God Herself. Everybody loved Beanie, from the newest arrival to God the Mother, God the Daughter, and God the Holy Ghost, who circled around Beanie's head flapping her white wings and cooing.

Also Beanie was quick at catching prayers. He snapped prayers out of the air like flies, prayers for help, prayers of thanks, prayers for forgiveness, you name it, Beanie caught it. Then he trotted daintily over to the prayer bin and dropped them in for God to sort out and answer, or not. They were quite a team. Of course God didn't have to do all that prayer-sorting Herself. She had the whole angel industry backing Her up, but She took a personal interest in prayer processing. In fact, God was doing a quality-control check one day when She found one that touched Her heart.

"Dear God," said the prayer, "I have no mother or father or sisters or brothers, and all the kids in the orphanage hate me. So does my teacher. You know all this stuff already, but what you might not have figured out is I need a friend. Please send me a friend. Amen."

Beanie had already sailed off to catch prayers, with a whole fleet of baby angels chasing his tail. Naturally they learned how to catch prayers this way in no time at all—every soul in Heaven knew that playing was the best kind of education. God looked at the prayer again and grabbed Her C.E.O. (Chief Everlasting Officer, if you don't know) by the tip of one feathery wing. "Hey, Dale, who is this, anyway?"

"Oh, Lord, You know I don't keep all that stuff in my head. We've got a couple small wars going on down there, plus a lot of fighting in the streets, natural disasters on a global scale, and so many personal catastrophes I was up all night."

"Anything religious?"

"Just the usual, Christians versus Jews, Catholics versus Protestants, Hindus versus Muslims, etc. The Buddhists try to stay out of it. We haven't had time to check on the smaller denominations." He glanced anxiously up at a bank of oversized TV monitors. Fleets of angels passed into and out of the screens.

"Well, run this one through the computer."

"You want a full background check?"

"Might as well. Give me a printout, too. My e-mail account is overdrawn. I can hardly keep track anymore, the way things keep speeding up."

Dale looked at God closely. "You do look a little drawn," he said. "Maybe you need a break, Lord."

"Everybody needs a break, Dale. And this kid needs a friend. I don't know how things got so stacked up against him."

Dale looked at God over his glasses.

"Okay, I know what you're thinking. It's my fault. Maybe it's time I did take a break. I haven't had a vacation since the Ice Age, and look what happened then." God called Beanie and went off to have a little think. Beanie ducked behind a bush, ditched the baby angels, and came tearing after God. Every step he ran, his tiny back legs lifted like a pony kicking up the green pastures. God scooped him up on one arm. "You know it and I know it, Beanie. Everybody needs a friend, at least one." Beanie wagged his ratty tail, and God headed for the library. It was a personal library but open to the public except for one room, which had a big comfy chair, a deep comfy couch, a computer table, and a desk. The desk was piled high with books, well thumbed, but God reached into a little cubbyhole and pulled out a pack of cards. Somebody had given Her a nice pack of cards with Chihuahuas on them, for a joke, probably, but she used them all the time.

To tell the truth, God had her best thoughts playing solitaire. It cleared Her mind somehow, created a little space from the cares of the world. She won a lot. You wouldn't say that God cheated, exactly, but She could see right through all the cards and She kept a sharp eye out. She had pretty sharp eyes for an old lady, generally speaking, even though She claimed that all the e-mail was straining them. Plus, her back and neck hurt and She had to wear braces for carpal tunnel syndrome. But solitaire got Her away from all that, not solitaire on the computer screen, God forbid, but just the plain old-fashioned kind. She shuffled and dealt out a row of seven cards. The hand She'd dealt out was quite a challenge, and for a while She was busy putting this card on top of that one, singling out the aces, and so on. None of this kept Her from nattering on.

"You know, Beanie, we better ramble on down there. It's been a while, and I like to keep my hand in. Where is it in the Bible that says God knows about the fall of the sparrow and so on? I can't keep my own verses straight." God's voice-recognition software kicked in, and the screen flickered: Matthew 10:29–31; *see also* Luke 1:6–7. She peered through her bifocals. "That's it," She muttered to Beanie. Then She neatly stacked up all the diamonds, hearts, clubs, and spades. She stared out the window at infinite green pastures, feeling rested and refreshed. "Come on, baby, are you ready to go? How shall we do this—maybe the homeless street person." God opened the closet and changed Her spotless white robe for a dirty old pink blouse, an orange-and-purple plaid skirt, a green sweater, a brown coat, rundown sneakers with no socks, and a regulation navy watch cap. Her gray curls stuck out every which way. Beanie sniffed the shoes curiously. "God knows where these shoes have been, Beanie, but I don't want to think about it." Last of all She grabbed a cane, just in case. You had to be careful down there.

"Now where's Dale's report?" The moment

❖184❖

she spoke, God's printer spit out a brief memo. It wasn't very long—the prayer had pretty much summed things up—but there were some necessary details of time, place, person. God turned on the TV, flicked the channel to the orphanage, and studied the situation for a minute or two. She didn't like what She saw, but you had to be there, smell things, touch things, to really tell. There were energy currents around people, between people, that you couldn't pick up online. God took a deep breath and disappeared into the screen, with Beanie peeking out of an old shopping bag full of rags.

They landed at a deserted bus stop right by the orphanage. It was cold. God had forgotten how cold Chicago got in December. The wind swept off the lake like a Siberian labor camp. She wished She could forget about Siberian labor camps. They were supposed to be over now. She had done Her best under the circumstances. Humans made their own circumstances, and God had to deal with them. Thank the Lord She had put on this old coat. Beanie was shivering, so She wrapped him up deeper in the little nest of rags. Then She looked up and down the deserted street. Not a human or angel in sight, just trash blowing around the sidewalk like tumbleweed. She looked up at the gray concrete building that called itself an orphanage. Speaking of Siberian labor camps. She made her way along the wire fence, pulled a set of universal master keys out of her pocket, and opened up the front gate. No point in picking the lock if you didn't have to. Jail was not her mission tonight. She crossed the barren playground and went around back. There was a light in one window. Everything else was dark. Raggedy clouds scuttered across the night sky. God tried a couple more keys and slipped in the back door.

She climbed the stairs, pressed against a wall to avoid the squeaking floorboards. When they came to the third door on the right down the hallway, God saw two sets of bunk beds. Each one had a child huddled down under a blanket, but none of them looked warm enough, maybe never would be. She tiptoed over, set down Her bag, and tucked in a sheet hanging down off the top bunk. Framed between the slats of a railing that kept the child from rolling out of bed was a face right beside Her own, a plain skinny face, none too clean, looking in desperate need of a friend. God peered at each of the other sleepers. None of these was the answer to a prayer for friendship. Even at this age, they had been shown no mercy and would give none. Children were very straightforward that way.

God picked up the bag, stroked Beanie's bony little head, and made Her way down the hall. None of these rooms seemed to offer any realistic possibilities. They radiated loneliness and preemptive defense against loneliness. Then she came to the lighted room. At first God thought it was empty. She saw a row of tables with chairs turned upside down on top, a wall lined with blackboards, a wall lined with bulletin boards. There was a fish tank, a terrarium, an ant colony—some possibilities here, but none of them human. Then She saw the teacher, head resting on arms resting on desk. God couldn't see her face, so She looked into her head. The teacher was dreaming. God could see through dreams like a pack of cards. The teacher was dreaming that all Hell had broken out in the classroom, quite a bit like the situation that had developed yesterday, in fact. God remembered a stray spitball flying all the way to Heaven on an updraft. The teacher was not bad-hearted, but she was young and inexperienced. The children were not bad-hearted, either, but they were experienced.

The noise rose to a new level in the dream, just as it did all the time in real life. Everybody in the room was in motion except for one child, who stared miserably out the window. The teacher raised her voice higher and higher to outbid them and was close to shouting explanations of a math problem on the blackboard. A scuffle broke out among four rough boys in the back row, and others began watching closely, choosing sides, placing bets. She knew she must stop the fight before it got violent, but the boys were bigger than she was and she didn't know how. The director had given her a warning only days before. If he walked in now, she would be fired. Maybe that would be best. None of the ideals she had brought from teacher training worked with actual children. A secretarial job looked like Heaven from where she stood. Suddenly the boy who had been staring out the window closed his eyes, folded his hands, and bent his head as if in prayer. The insolence of it, the implication that only God could get this classroom back into control, shook her into a rage. Her hands were actually shaking as she stalked toward him, the one child she knew she could control, the one whose eyes stared accusations of defeat at her hour after hour, day after day. She had one of those shaking hands raised to strike him when the principal opened the door and the dream ended.

God knew that the actual situation hadn't gone quite as far as the dream (the principal hadn't opened the door), but it was getting perilously close. God also knew that there were strict rules about Heavenly intervention. It had to be subtle. You couldn't just go working miracles all the time. Nobody would believe them, to start with, and then the more common they got, the more people would take them for granted, and how could she up the ante on a miracle? But God was nothing if not subtle. Just as the teacher began to wake up, trying to keep from being fired in her dream before it really happened, God simply glided over to the wall and turned off the light.

The teacher experienced the lightbulb going off like some people experience a lightbulb going on, like an idea flooding the brain. Her mind, muddled by the dream, experienced the light going off as a continuation of the dream, which extended to a silent, peaceful classroom flooded with moonlight. How could she have fallen asleep here? Easily, after three weeks of insomnia, after working late to try and stave off the next day, to generate enough work to fend off the class from final revolt. She gathered herself shakily and prepared to stumble up to her own room in the staff quarters, while God and Beanie retreated to a park bench for a nap.

The next day started badly, as usual. The teacher couldn't seem to sort out her days from her nightmares anymore. It all happened again, like echoes coming faster and louder rather than slower and fainter. If you read the dream carefully, you'll find the next bit déjà vu, just as the teacher felt it. (Of course, God's feelings of déjà vu are eternal.) The noise rose to a new level. Everybody in the room was in motion except for the one child, who always stared miserably out the window. The teacher raised her voice higher and higher to outbid them and was close to shouting explanations of a math problem on the blackboard. The usual scuffle broke out among four rough boys in the back row, and others began watching closely, choosing sides, placing bets. She knew she must stop the fight before it got violent, but the boys were bigger than she was and she didn't know how. She remembered once more the warning that the director had given her only days before. If he walked in now, she would be fired. Suddenly the boy closed his eyes, folded his hands, and bent his head as if in prayer. The insolence of it, the implication that only God could get this classroom back into control, shook her into a savage rage. Her hands were actually shaking as she stalked toward him, the one child she knew she could control, the one whose eyes stared accusations of defeat at her hour after hour, day after day.

Yes, it was all desperately familiar. She knew what was going to happen next, knew the principal would be coming down the hall, but she couldn't stop herself. She was approaching the boy, hand up to strike him, when she remembered the very end of the dream.

Her eyes leaped to the light switch on the wall, and she changed direction, walking over to it, switching it off, and suddenly enveloping the room with a soft gray blanket of darkening wintry afternoon. The noise stopped immediately. The children looked in amazement, first at her, then out the window at the source of tranquillity. When the room fell quiet, the teacher fell quiet. When she spoke again, she spoke in a quiet voice. The children listened. The boy looked up at her and smiled. It was the first time she had ever seen him smile, and she smiled back. At that moment the door opened and the director looked in.

"Just checking," he said brusquely. "I heard a lot of noise coming from here a few minutes ago."

She smiled at the principal, too. "We're practicing," she said, "loud and soft, light and dark." The children looked at her in further amazement. It was the first thing they had ever learned here. They liked it. The principal withdrew his head, and the teacher walked confidently to the front of the room. "All right, children," she said softly. "We're going to practice these math problems for a while and then turn the lights back on and practice your band instruments." She looked at her watch. "You have ten minutes to finish these. On your mark, get set, go!" Paper rustled, pencils scribbled and broke. The quiet child, finishing first, waved his hand gladly in the air.

That night God didn't really have to return to the scene—She knew things had gone pretty well—but She couldn't resist. So many things didn't turn out well, no matter what She did. Some humans just didn't get it, or wouldn't, or couldn't. The teacher got it. But God wanted to check on that boy. She slipped into the room with the bunk beds and tucked the blanket up around his thin shoulders. Beanie poked his head out of the shopping bag. Then he jumped delicately onto the bed and licked the boy's hand, like the touch of a feather, without waking him up. God looked at Beanie, Beanie looked at God, and the tiny dog curled up next to the boy for keeps. God didn't want to lose Beanie's company, but She had to answer that prayer.

There was certainly no occasion for a miracle.

God knew the rules about unnatural intervention, and yet She just felt so *righteous* at that moment. You couldn't say God cheated exactly, but it's a fact that the room filled with a divine light that put electricity to shame, and the sleeping boy's face shone. Without even knowing it, God works in mysterious ways.

+HE DEVIL
AND +HE DOG

The dog just wouldn't let go. It was long since dead, like its wicked owner, whom the Devil had had no trouble disposing of in the usual way—body ditched, soul collected and deposited in the smoldering garbage dump of damnation. Of course, the dog's body was easy to hack away. All but the teeth, or rather the grip. The teeth seemed to have an eternal life of their own. The Devil did not believe that animals had souls, but if they did, this animal's soul was all teeth. The Devil couldn't actually see them, but clearly something was crunching on his skin, bunching up his pants leg, and dragging him back. It complicated walking considerably, not to mention flying. Swimming, which the Devil avoided unless

caught up in chasing some panic-stricken resist-
ant sinner, was impossible.

The Devil was strong, but this situation was
wearing him down. It was also embarrassing.
The Devil's face scared most folks too much for
them to detect any oddity in his lower body area,
but naturally his wife noticed right away, so he
had to confess. "Just don't pass it around your
gossip league," he growled, knowing immediately that this was the wrong thing to say. She
didn't get to be the Devil's wife for nothing.

Going to bed was out of the question. For
one thing, he couldn't get his pants off that one
leg with the teeth pulling them tight, and for
another, his wife put her foot down when it
came to sleeping with an active set of teeth lung-
ing this way and that between the sheets. She
made him sleep on the couch. Unfortunately,
the teeth never slept. They were in a state of per-
petual bite, punctuated now and then by an
ominous and throaty growl, throaty because of
the amount of trouser muting the sound. As
fatigue set in, the Devil got distracted from his
work. A significant dimension of Hell's torment
is overpopulation. Just when you're choking on

screaming souls, another load piles on top of you. If you're not suffocating, you're not suffering. The Devil was exhausted, but he needed to up the ante before the population made peace with its current space allowance and noise level. Perpetually escalating agony was the whole point.

"What have you tried, to get him off?" asked his wife.

"Everything," said the Devil. "Kicking, beating, instruments of torture . . . and it's a her."

The Devil's wife smirked. "How about being nice?" she suggested. "They say dogs respond to that."

"Who says?" growled the Devil.

"Oh, you know, the good guys."

The Devil scowled at her. "What have you been up to?" He swung his fist with the intention of bludgeoning her surgically beautified face but missed—the dog held him back just enough to let her scoot away.

"Wouldn't you like to know," she taunted him, and ran out the door.

The Devil sat down as best he could on the kitchen stool and lit a cigarette. The click of the gold lighter shot him full of inspiration. He of all creatures should have thought of burning the damn thing. With considerable relish he pushed the cigarette at the bunched-up cloth of his pants leg. Once, twice, thrice . . . scorched circles dotted the fabric, but the pressure on his leg did not ease. He grabbed the lighter, flicked it on, and bore down on the teeth. There was a yowl— not from the dog, but the Devil, as his skin sizzled through a blackened patch of gabardine. All the ghostly logistics he'd used in his own hounding of humanity were working against him. The Devil hurled the gold lighter across the room. The tiny flame instantly caught hold of the Devil's wife's orange polyester curtains, which roared into action energetically enough to reach the propane gas tank under her new Hercules range. The ensuing explosion would have made pyrotechnic history on earth.

Now it's true that flame is Hell's signature medium, but the Devil enjoys roasting a good deal more than getting roasted, not to mention getting faced with his wife's reaction to the incineration of their newly renovated kitchen. The mini-inferno was hopelessly out of control. For obvious reasons, there's no fire department in Hell. The minute he smashed the window and climbed out—his dog-tugged leg scraping on the jagged glass—there she was, raging and hurling curses in his singed wake. The Devil coughed up a good deal of smoke, retreated to his den of iniquity across town, and brooded. Throughout his ordeal the teeth had only increased their grip, while the howls of Hell were decreasing steadily in pitch and degree of agitation.

"Look," he said finally to the teeth. Then he got caught up in the difficulty of teeth looking. The Devil prided himself on disputation.

"All right then, listen." Same problem, but he had to start somewhere. For the first time, the Devil began to regret killing something.

"I'm sorry, okay? I should have left you up there."

The teeth stayed clamped.

The Devil took a deep breath. "Nice dog," he wheedled. "Nice, nice doggy." The Devil groped around his pants leg and gave a tentative pat. He leaned back a little, closed his eyes, and stroked whatever there was to stroke. God, he was tired. The Devil's eyes closed. In a dreamy state he realized that the teeth had started loosening up. The Devil smiled a little to himself and continued stroking. Maybe he should relax more often. Maybe he should get a dog. Well, no, he had a dog, sort of.

The Devil sighed, and from that day on, things changed. You wouldn't call it a transformation exactly, but every once in a while, the living and dead got just a little respite, because when the Devil starts running too hard, those teeth clamp down again until he slows his pace. You can always count on a dog. That's what the good guys say, anyway.